THE WALLBOYS

if this wall could talk

D1520024

J A M A R L   R A Y

ISBN: 1517071763
ISBN 13: 9781517071769

PROLOGUE

Sometimes I wonder what it would be like to be born into a worry free environment. I guess no environment is truly worry free but **I know there are kids out here that never had or never will have to worry about the things I had to worry about. You know what I mean, kids born with their mom and dad well off in a fortune five hundred company or something. When on their 16th birthday there's a fly ride waiting for them in the driveway. I know it's said that everybody has a** choice and yada yada yada...let me tell you the first real choice I remember making. It was at the age of 12 and I had the choice of going to live with my grandmother or going to stay at a foster home until someone may or may not have come and adopted me. At this time my moms pregnant with her forth child on the way, they're already questioning her capabilities of raising the three she has and here comes another blessing. Now at this time my parents addiction had reached a all time low or should I say "high" long story short the state swooped in I went to stay with my granny and my five and seven year old brothers went to stay with my aunt. Now my grandmother lived in the projects but it wasn't your average project house, her lawn was fenced in and well taken care of with a garden that bordered the base of the yard. My granddad worked for a construction company so he made pretty good money which showed through the furnishings in the house. It had big screen T.V's plush carpet and a moderately expensive living room set, and they kept me draped in the latest fashion out of Macy's boys department. This was a big change from the environment I just came from. I wouldn't say my mom had a crack house, it was more of a funhouse if anything. My moms and dads drug use allowed them to have carefree attitudes as long as the kids weren't bleeding we didn't get much attention. My cousins and uncles were hustlers so they were in and out of my moms house gambling and drinking. I would steal a marijuana joint out of the ashtray or a wine cooler out of the fridge and go and smoke or drink with my friends. So being a part of this lifestyle infused it into my system so when I moved in with my granny in a more civilized environment it lacked the excitement I was use to, I guess that played a part in how I got addicted to the streets. I had a few friends near my granny's house but they were goody two shoes so to speak so I could only do so much with them. They got into an occasional scuffle but nothing to serious but when I would hang with my friends from my mothers block we were always into something. We went to the white boys neighborhood to steal trick bikes then would sell them to the neighborhood hustlers which started to build a bond between us and the hustlers. We started doing little odd jobs for them, go pick this up or take this to such and such, sometimes they would have a couple of us jump a fiend that owed them money or ruff up some lil kids they were too old to put hands on. We idolized the hustlers and would pretty much do anything for them, so I spent most of my free time up with my two sets of friends about 20% with my goody 2 shoes friends and the other 80% with my hoodlum friends or atleast thats what my granny calls them. I began to notice that even though I did what the rest of my hoodlum friends did with the exception of disrespecting elders! I now realize that it most likely comes from spending time or being raised rather from age 12 on up in a civilized enviroment. When I visited alot of friends its pure chaos, so they were neglected that experience of a civilized home. So im spending my freetime wilding out with my hoodlum friends but on a school night im home by 9:30 to shower, eat dinner and watch a couple of t.v. shows with my granny. So it was like living a double life and at the age of twelve thats probably not good because thats the age when you began to find yourself and I was discovering two differrent people and this went on for most of my teenage years. Here I have my grandfather showing me how to hold down a household, how important family is and how a man needs to work. Then I got the hustlers showing me how to hold down a block, how important your click is and to be the man you need "the work". So now im seventeen and full of two differrent sets of values thats been getting instilled in me for the past 5 years. I began to notice I could adapt to different settings that my peers couldn't. I could sit on the block and have a conversation with the older women who lived in front of the apartment, I would take thier trash out for them then serve a couple of sales behind the dumpster and come back and kick it with the older ladies like nothing happend. Now I don't know if having both of these identities is a gift or a curse. The streets teach you lessons that you can only learn in the streets and my grandfather taught me lessons in family values and things of that nature. So as I grew older I learned to survive in the streets you can't have a conscience and as i progressed from a teen to a man my conscience became stronger. I had a child and I grew feelings and an appeciation for life but mischief was implanted so deep in me that i was at a constant war with myself. So I present to you my war, my story, "THE WALLBOYS"!

CHAPTER 1'S INTRO

January 25th 2001 this was one crazy day. It was really like the sequel to the day before, so let me take you there first. Im in the tenth grade at the time and im the only one in my click who still goes to school but anyway im getting off the bus that brings me back to my neighborhood and who do I see? Well who do I hear rather, BAAAAANNNNNTTT BAAANNNNNTTT, BAAANNTING up the street? Fezie, on a dirtbike! This nigga don't even know how to ride but I must say he doing a pretty good job BAAANNNNNTTTT, BAAAAAAANNNNNNNNNNTTT!!!

Right past me, "oh yeah" fuck going home to drop my books off im going straight to the block. It took me every bit of two minutes to complete a five minute walk, I was walking with the "dope stroke". Oh if you don't know what the dope stroke is, its the fast paced walk that fiends and addicts…(I don't wanna say junkies) but anyway its the fast paced walk they walk with when there in a rush to copp (copp= buy drugs or anything for that matter) and there always in a rush to copp. Anyway I get to the block and this is whats happening.

CHAPTER 1
A day before forever!

___

Jan. 24, 2001

"You learned how to ride now all you gotta do is learn how to look left and right so you will see ya man flaggin you down." I said as Fezie came around the corner of the apartment building, bikeless! "I saw you but the police bust a u (u=u-turn) on Bethune. So I wasn't stopping for you, stop signs, red lights or nothing. "You see I put the bike up", Fezie says a little out of breathe. "Who's bike is that anyway, and when you learn how ta ride?" I asked! "Thats P shit he bought it last night right after you left for real; him and O bought it up here on the back of a pick-up, tell Manna teach you how to ride. Just wait though cuz me and Manna took it out of P yard this mornin and I know he bouta get off work at three" Fezie informed me. "Nigga it's 3:20 and P ready come up here flipping. Look there he go right there, he walkin wit the dope stroke too." "Yo! who went in my yard?" P yelled as Manna and Fezie looked at him with the dumb high look on their faces, so he continued searching for answers. "Where the fuck is my bike at?" P said agressively. "You act like a nigga stole ya shit or somethin, ya fuckin bike is in da fuckin building. If I had a bike an was at work all day yall could rockout! Fezie said while crossing his arms making his point.

"That ain't the point, ain't none of yall goin pay for my shit if the police take it."

"Pay for it, pay for it? Its jammin out this bitch." Manna boasted while grabbing knots of money out of his front pockets.

"Like I said that ain't the point, yall goin all in a nigga yard while im at work an shit! Like yall sayin fuck a nigga forreal."

"Whoa...Whoa...come on now P wit all that extra shit. Niggaz just had gas on their chest!" I say trying to mediate.

"Man fuck that bike!" Fezie zaps, "he wanna act funny wit his bike; fuck that bike. Im glad you up here Scotty, I saw a four wheeler this morning on my way out here. I know your grandfather got some bolt cutters down there all them tools an shit he got!"

"Yeah, most likely he got some," I answered Fezie.

"Yeah get them, we goin get that four wheeler tonight!"

"Where its at? You know my tags ain't right," Manna says.

"Its right between Cherry Hill and Westport behind..."Fezie begins to explain then zaps. "What diffrence it make, you ride everywhere else on them fucked up tags."

(Baaannnntt, Bannnnnnttt!!!...P comes around the corner reving his bike.)

"Whatchu bouta take the bike in the house? What the fuck you buy it for if you ain't goin ride da mufucka? "Manna asked.

"I be back," P said before riding off.

"Imma run down my house an drop these books off an shit," I said to nobody in particular.

"Oh that's my girl right there; black tops how many baby?" Fezie asked an approaching fien.

"Naw red tops baby, if you pass me by you won't get high!" Manna says to the same fiend.

"Who goin give me 12 for a hunnit" the fiend asked?

"12 for a hunnit all day", manna said on his cut-throat shit.

"How about both of yall give me six for fifty"

(Manna and Fezie both go to their stashes.)

"Hey handsome; you all on the block wit ya school books on an shit. I know thats right, stay in school nephew: education first. This block goin be here," the lady fiend says as a male fiend approaches.

"Give me four shorty, I got thirty eight; is that cool?"

"Yeah, I guess, ay yo! Both of yall bring two more," I yell to Manna and Fezie while they're still at there stashes.

"Shorty don't hustle!" The lady fiend tells the dude.

"Danm nephew, my bad. I seen the books I jus thought you was fakin the police out."

"Here baby", Fezie says while handing the lady 6 glass vials filled with white rocks. "These two for you unk," Fezie adds talking to the man.

"Yeah I want four, I got 38," shorty said it was cool."

"Yeah give me the money, "Fezie tells him as Manna approaches and gave 6 red topped vials to the lady.

"These other two for you unk?" Manna asked!

"Yeah; I gave Black the money already."

"Here manna: he had 18," Black says. "Yeah aight, next time you takin the short."

" Damn yall made all that this morning?" I asked as manna and fezie added the fiends money to the knots of money they pulled out of their pockets.

"Yeah I think mufuckas started gettin income tax money or somethin cuz its been jammin out this bitch," fezie says.

"Man fuck that! Do you got any high school bitches for us," Manna cuts in.

"Scotty ain't got no bitches, he in love wit Angie," Fezie says.

"How long you been fuckin wit that girl?" Manna asked!

"She walked past here the other day, she gettin a lil phat too. I almost hollered at her til I seen her face," Fezie said with a chipped tooth smile.

"Forreal, she ain't come ta school today! I probably go check on her before I come back up here."

"Don't forget the wire cutters," Fezie reminds me.

"Yeah yeah..im not goin forget, let me get outta here though I be back around seven."

I went home and checked on granny and she was watching T.V in the living room as usual. I dropped my books off and grabbed a quick snack then told granny I was going down Angie's. As I was leaving out my father was coming in, "Daddy let me holla atchu right quick," I tell him before he gets all the way in the house. Out front I break it down simply, real quick.

"Where does granddaddy keep his wire cutters/bolt cutters or whatever can cut a chain?" My father told me he had a pair, so I asked him to drop them off up the wall before 6. And he said he would, "solid," I said bumped his fist then proceeded to Angie's house.

So im down Angie's checking on my shorty and she is sick as a dog. I guess she can't handle this winter weather cuz her nose is stopped up, she keeps sneezing and complaining that her head hurts. So im not tryna play her too close cuz I don't wanna get sick next. I told her that im gonna find a ride to the store/shopping center and get her some soup, tea, halls....the whole works! Then (baaaaaaaaaaannnnnnnnnntttttt, baaaaannnnnnnnt!!!)

"OH MY GOD", she yells! "That noise feels like its right inside my head. What the fuck, is the nigga riding his dirt bike in my yard or something?", she says not really to me; just venting I guess!

"Yeah that shit do sound like its right outside, let me go tell whoever it is to take that bike somewhere." But just as soon as I say it the bike shuts off and I hear Fezie yell up at the window. "Ay Scotty...Aye Scotty, take ya face out it and come to the window."

"He a ignorant motherfucker," she says.

"You know I seen his black ass the other day when I was walking past the wall, he talkin bout put him on wit somebody."

"Ayy Scotty!!! "I know you in there," he yells again.

"Don't pay him no mind he got lead, let me go see what he want tho. Matter of fact imma get him to ride me up the store, jus call it in," I tell her as I leave the room.

"Yo why the fuck you blowin my spot up like that? What if her mufa was in there? You talkin bout get your face out it, wuts up tho?" I say as I slap hands wit my nigga.

"Shit, P bought the bike back out. I told em you was tryna learn how to ride," he said!

"Lets grab some grass and go down the field, I got 6 for 50 off of Bethune. You ready now or you goin meet us down the field?" he asked.

"Naw im ready," I say as I hop on back of the bike, then telling him..

"Yo don't do none of that extra shit! No fishtales, no wheelies or none of that extra shit just ride!"

We get up the wall without any incidents, I get off the back of the bike and show all my niggaz love.

"Whats up O, wut it do Lil Greezy? Let me hit that weed Poka I ain't been high allday! P its good ta see you got off that bullshit and bought the bike back out."

"Fuck you, put some gas in this mufucka," P says.

I was about to ask Manna did my father come up here but he was to busy grabbing the bike from Fezie and revving it up so it doesn't shut off. That's when Poka tapped me while choking, holding the blunt out for me to grab out of his hand.

"See bean over, he went in the building to grab another pack. He should be ready to spin the bin," Poka says.

"Aight yo, they not lettin you come back ta school?" I ask Poka as I hit the blunt.

"Man, they tryna have a meeting with me and my mother down the board of education and blah blah blah, fuck that shit im gettin money I ain't wit all that extra shit."

"How the fuck they catch you wit a pack on you anyway?"

"That dirty bitch twin tells the school police I got her 400 degrees tape, so they come to my class on some bullshit. And im high as shit at the time smelling like a pound, so the coon get slick wit me. One thing led to another and they cuff me for assault on the rent a cop. Thats when they checked me and found the pills, I ain't even goin lie I forgot them pills was in my pocket. I had them fatigues on wit all them danm pockets, I wasn't even thinkin forreal."

"Where that blunt at Poka?" Bean yells as he turns the corner.

"I got it right here Bean, jus let me hit it a couple more times i jus got it," I tell him.

"Whats up Scotty? I jus saw ya father around the corner with a big as pair of sissors or somethin, there he go right there." Bean said.

"Ay Big Scotty let me see dem mufuckas," Fezie says jumping off The Wall he was sitting on." Yeah these look like they will work! I ain't see the lock but these look like they will snap a ankle clean off" Fezie says opening the cutters back and forth.

"Who got the black tops," a fiend says walking towards us.

"Right here unk," Fezie says, then he goes on to ask.. "I will give you a whole pack if you let me cut your ankle off with these?"

"Shorty you outta ya mufuckin mind," the fiend responds.

"Aight, well I will give you ten free pills if you let me snap off ya pinky finger?"

"Nephew im jus tryna get three black tops, im not tryna get my finger or my ankle cut off.

"O run me up the store right fast?" I asked as I see him walking off.

"Come on shorty the car in the parking lot," he responds.

"I don't see the Q (Q-45), I say", as we approached the parking lot.

"Oh I traded that shit in, I got the Ac now!"

"Oh yeah, burgundy TL with the dipped rims. Yeah this joint clean," I say admiring O's new ride.

O took me up the store and down my girls house to drop her stuff off. We never made it to the field, Manna got chased by the police on the bike so P put it up for the day and we just got high until it was time to go and steal the four wheeler.

"Park in the parking lot Manna, we goin come thru the back. It's a alley that lead right to the house," Fezie instructed.

"What time is it Bean?"

"Its 10:51, why?"

"Im jus asking, pop the trunk so I can grab the wire cutters!"

"Do yall see it? It's right there on the side of the house, that blanket is over top of it."

"Yeah," we all respond to Fezie's question.

"Give me the bolt cutters Scotty!"

"Here Fezie, im about to run around front and make sure ain't no lights on in the living room....yeah they out! Hurry up lets do this," I say while rubbing my hands together.

"I almost got it," Fezie whispers." It's only one link left, here Bean pop the last link I gotta take a piss."

"Hold on, the upstairs light jus came on duck down Fezie." I say as the rest of us lean against the side of the house.

"Ayy, what chall doin in my yard?" A female asks as she stuck her head out of the window and saw the rest of us. Then she began to yell, Jimmy!! They tryna steal ya fourwheeler, get the fuck out my yard! Jimmmy!!!!"

"Fuck you and jimmy bitch!" Manna yells.

"Come on lets get the fuck outta here," I say as we all start to make a break towards the alley.

As soon as we get to the end of the alley all you hear is.....POP! PA! PA! POP! POP!! POP!!! POP!!!!

CHAPTER 2'S INTRO

The next morning Tyrod called me a little after 9:00 AM. It was a Saturday so I was in the house. Tyrod, me and shorty are like brothers. He's a year older than me but that shit don't matter, he seen the G in me when he took me on my first mission and every since then we been rolling like dice. Long story short I introduced him to The Wallboys! O liked him and started giving him packs and I guess thats when he officially became a Wallboy. Anyway it's 9 something in the morning and he is on the phone asking me to hit the block with him. He seen me hesitating to say yeah so he baits me in by telling me he got something to holla at me about..Oh yeah and he got some grass so I was sold!

Me and T-Rod get up The Wall around 10, Manna and Fezie are already there posted up at the stop sign smoking a blunt. We all slap hands T-Rod tells me to roll the weed up while he goes to stash his pills.

CHAPTER 2
Gone 4 Eva!

"T-Rod did niggaz tell you Fezie almost got us killed lastnight?" I asked.

"Man that nigga was bluffin he must was shooting in the air or something." Fezie says.

"I don't know, I jus got the fuck outta there I didnt look back and all yall niggaz was beside me," I say as I dry the blunt with my lighter.

Tyrod jumps in saying; "Yo, who the fuck shot at chall? Do I know the nigga, do he know my face? If not I can walk down on em!"

"Jus chill, imma bake a cake for that nigga!" Fezie says while rubbing his hands together like baby.

"I hear that shit Biatrice," I say sarcastically to Fezie.

"Im tryna ride," Manna says as he passes the blunt to T-Rod.

"Yo I said imma take care of that shit!" Fezie says as he starts to get mad (mostly at himself).

"Im talkin bout the bike, I already know we goin handle that shit from lastnight!" Manna says looking at the stretch of road ahead of him.

"Yeah im still tryna learn how ta ride," I say to Manna mostly.

"I'll teach you, you know imma fool wit it." He responds.

"Man you know O talked niggas heads off about that shit lastnight and im not tryna sit through another one of those speeches!" I say.

"We jus goin take the bike and put it back before P get off work," Manna says. Then tells Fezie to come on as he heads in the direction of P's house.

Baaaaaaaannnnnttttt!! Baaaaaaaaaaaaaaaaaaaaannnnnnnnnnnnttt!!!! Fezie comes riding past with Manna on the back of the bike," we will be right back!" Manna yells as him and Fezie ride (Baaaaaaaaannnt) past us.

"You know how ta ride?" I ask as me and T-Rod stand at the stop sign! (If I need to explain: T-Rod, Tyrod and T-Riggy are the same person!)

"Yeah I know how ta ride! I don't know how ta wheelie and all that extra shit but I can ride though, where that weed at? Light that blunt!"

"You ain't gotta tell me twice, whatchu had ta holla at me bout tho or you was jus bullshittin ta get me out the house?"

"Naw, naw I was just going tell you O came ta holla at me last night and your name came up."

"Came up about what?"

"Nothin heavy, O fucks wit you forreal! He said you know how ta think, he was asking why you don't hustle with the rest of us he said you up here everyday anyway."

"I was asking myself the same shit! I know yall getting tired of givin me cheese cuz im tired of askin yall."

"Hell no that shit ain't nothing niggaz don't be trippin off that shit, but pass the blunt my nigga you dome'n."

"My bad I got caught up in the conversatation, here my nigga what else O say though?"

"That was it forreal, he tried ta talk my head off but I got outta there on em."

"He talked niggaz heads off last night about taking P bike out his yard"

"Yeah he mentioned somethin to me last night about that shit, but fuck that shit whatchu goin do?"

"Do about what?"

"Hustling nigg!"

"I don't know, Big Greezy tried ta get me ta hustle for him. I was thinkin bout it because he got his own coke and everybody else hustle for O."

"Man Grezzy goin try pimp you, I got a couple of packs from that nigga and he be on some shakey shit. That nigga got the right name Grezzy!"

"Man fuck that shit where the fuck dem niggaz at on that bike, they been gone for like ten minutes. I ain't heard the bike in the distance or nothin," I say looking down a empty round road.

"Here take this blunt, where the fuck is the money at? It's saturday it should be jammin up this bitch. Lets walk down the street an get Bean."

"Fuck it, come on!"

(Baaaaaaaaaaaaaaaannnnnnnnnnnnnnnnnntttt!!!!! Baaaaaaaaaaaaaaannnnn nnnnnnnnntttt!!!!!! Baaaaaaaaaaaaaaaaaaaaaaaaaaa...)

"There dem niggaz go right there," I say stating the obvious.

"They jus goin throw the hold up finger at us and keep goin," T-rod says with a little disappointment in his voice.

"Fuck that shit, lets go get Bean."

"Ay Bean! Ya da Bean head!" T-Rod yelled up at Beans window of his grandmother house about a half a block from The Wall.

"Jus throw a rock at window, fuck all that yelling!" I tell T-Rod.

"Boy you smart, O was right about you." T-Rod says being smart.

"Either that or you niggas jus dumb!" I say returning his sarcasim then recanting, "naw im jus fuckin wit you my nigga."

(Bean opens his window)

"Boy if you goin look like that when you wake up you don't need ta go ta sleep," I say as Bean sticks his head out the window.

"Fuck both yall!" Bean says yawning an stretching.

"What's up, you comin out?" T-Rod askes him.

"Yeah im bouta hop in the shower, I be out in bouta half."

"When the fuck you start takin showers?" T-rod ask jokingly.

"Yeah he on some new shit ain't he?" I say agreeing with T-Rod.

"Man fuck yall, get the fuck out my yard befor I air shit out like that bitch ass nigga did last night!" Bean says then shuts his window.

Me and T-Rod walk back to the stop sign and wait for Manna and Fezie to come back thru on the bike.

"There go a sale comin thru the hole," I tell t-rod and nod my head in the direction im talking about.

"About fuckin time," he complains then yells, "how many unk?"

"Man thats Manna, that ain't no sale!" I correct him.

"Well he look like a fuckin Unk walkin thru the hole wit the dope stroke."

"Yeah he is walkin like a Unk."

"Yo me and Fezie jus got chased by the police and he told me to get off the back of the bike so he can getaway. I think he fell or they hit em off the bike cuz I seen him on Cherryhill Road laid out with the bike layin next to him," Manna tells us nearly outta breath.

"Man them bitch ass police ain't even supposed ta be chasin bikes!" I say angrily.

"We gotta go down there," Manna says.

"There go Gipp flag his car down Scotty."

"Fuck Gipp, he don't fuck wit me after I fucked that weed money up, you flag em down T-Riggy."

"What's up lil niggas?" Gipp asked thru his window after T-rod stopped his car.

"Run us on Cherryhill Road?" Manna ask cutting the small talk.

"Get in!" Gipp replys.

As we get to the the sight of the crash we see Fezie laying still in the street with a paramedic rubbing from his chest to his stomach. Fezie looks a little scraped up but I don't see any serious injuries. After about a minute of the paramedic rubbing from his chest to his stomach I hear the paramedic mumble to the police, "HE'S GONE!"

"HE'S WHAT!" I yell.

"Fuck no, come on Fezie!" Tyrod says standing next to me.

"Hell no, get up Fez come on g!" Manna pleads.

After about a minute or two of disbelief and cursing out the cops and paramedics reality sets in and like that he was gone, GONE 4 EVA.

CHAPTER 3'S INTRO

Everybody came together the morning of the funeral. Of course all of the Wallboys were there, the Wallgirls (Nikki, Grezzy, Ki-Ki, and Tywanda). The Slater girls were there (Jennifer, Jessica, Kelly, Sherell ect.).

Glenn's babymother Chardae and her home girls Marie and Nelly were also there. The Wallgirls, they all had us by a couple of years in age but they loved us like we were their younger brothers. You know that brother/sister relationship can lead to fucking under the right circumstances but it was love with us and the Wallgirls. It wasn't really a sexual thing we looked at each other like family. Now Glenn's babymother and her homegirls hated the Slater girls and the Slater girls hated them right back but for the sake of the day everybody co-exsisted with each other. So everyone's up the wall before the funeral talking, smoking, drinking, crying or just zoning out. We made plans to meet at Ki-Ki's house after the burial then we started to figure out who was riding with who. The slater girls ended up riding with O, Glenn's babymother and her homegirls rode with P-olie, me, Bean and T-rod rode with Ki-Ki and so on and so on. The whole ride to the funeral parlor Ki-Ki played the same song over and over

(Master P's 'I really miss my homies) **I use ta hang wit my boy/I use ta slang wit my boy/even bang wit my boy/ goddanm I miss my boy**.

Honestly I can't tell you much about the funeral because after the initial viewing of the body I took a seat and it felt like my head weighed a thousand pounds. I only found the strenght to lift it up twice.

Once when Fezie's grandmother spoke and when his nephew recited a poem he wrote for his uncle. After the burial we all met down Ki-Ki's house and O took center stage.

CHAPTER 3

The Funeral

"Look, I know yall say I talk yall head off with my speeches but I feel like its my duty as a real nigga to educate yall with the shit I already know and have been thru. This might not be the best time or yall might not want to hear this right now but yall need to hear it. When yall took P's bike"....

"Stole, them niggas ain't take shit!" P cut O off with that correction then O continued on acknowledging P's correction.

"When yall stole P's bike the first time I told yall niggas yall was wrong for disrespecting that man like that and I told yall not to go back in his yard and...blah, blah, blah, blah!" That's what the shit sounded like to me when O went on for about an hour with it but we all sat there listening and not listening at the same time. It was something about O. It might of been a mix-up of facts but it coulda been we were young and in a influintial stage in our lives not to mention O was a street nigga but he was so well spoken kinda like president Obama. If you took the time to listen he made you believe in what ever he was saying. So he's in the middle of our huddle wearing some 300 dollar black Moschino pants with white pinstripes on them, a black Moschino muscle shirt or maybe it just looked like a muscle shirt because it wasen't oversized like most people's clothes in 2001 but anyway I turned my attention from him to Manna who I could tell was taking Fezie's death extra hard. Probably because it was his idea to go and get the bike outta P's yard. Now im not good at giving words of encourgement to grieving people but this is my nigga so I gotta say something.

"Pick your head up soldier," I say to Manna as I take a seat next to him and began talking.

"Yo I remember the day I met Fezie, we were in the 5th grade and you know our first names are the same. So we use to hear each others names over the intercom everyday. Jamal report to the main office, Jamal please report to the principle's office, everyday we use to hear each others name but we never saw each other. Until one day we bumped heads in the principals office together and im saying to myself..this the nigga who got my name and he must was thinking the same thing cuz he looked up and said.. so you the other Jamal? You my fuckin son boy. That summer my mother moved up The Wall right next door to Fezie. That's when he introduced me to all of yall and the rest was history." This at least got a smile out of Manna as he must have begun to think back a couple of years.

"Ay yall, Glenn on the phone," Ki-Ki came into the living room announcing with the phone in one hand and a cup of liquor in the other.

"Let me holla at him!" Manna says jumping off the couch and snatching the phone from Ki-Ki's hand.

"What's up Lil G, when you comin home nigga? The streets miss you," Manna says excitedly thru the phone.

"It should be real soon, they just threw my gun charge out so now I should be able to get a bail for the drug charge," Glenn answers back thru the phone then ask.."how yall niggas doin tho? Thats fucked up about Fezie, you know that was my birthday he died on. Yo I ain't come out for rec or nothing I jus sat in my cell and smoked like 20 jelly rolls real shit I cried and all that shorty was my heart."

"Yeah that shit fucked all of us up," Manna responded.

"We pullin through tho, everybody send their love to you and the rest of yall niggaz behind the fence. You know everybody came down here after the funeral. I think your babymother out front smoking you want me to take the phone to her?" Manna said walking out of the living room.

"Jennifer let me have some of that cranberry juice, Poka chasa drinkin ass drank all my sprite an shit," I say as im filling a plastic cup up with Hennessy.

"Here you can have it," she replies.

"Jessica got another one, I will drink hers.

"Fill my cup up Scotty," Lil Grezzy says holding his cup out to me with only a sip of liquor left in it.

"Who did I give my box of dutches to?" Tyrod asked as he checked all of his pockets.

(This is basically how the day went, getting high and telling old stories about all the crazy shit Fezie use to do.)

CHAPTER 4'S INTRO

I say its about a week into Febuary and I come out of the school building. The whole school is out there about to get on the buses to take them to their neighborhoods. All the pretty bitches are out there, the seniors, the ballplayers, everybody. At this time im not really standing out;I mean I ain't ballin but I ain't bummin neither, im just ya average nigga. So im on my way to one of the school buses until I have to stop and ask myself "who keeps beeping that fuckin horn like they're crazy?" So I look left and see O standing outside of his T.L with his hands in the air, so I walk towards the car and I see Poka in the passenger seat putting the finishing touches on a blunt.

CHAPTER 4
(Is you down or what?)

"Let me get out this car so these hoes can see a nigga shinnin," Poka says stepping out of the car giving me a five (handshake) then saying. "Matter of fact where that bitch twin at? Imma ask her if she ever been smacked wit a stack, if not its her lucky day cuz imma smack her wit my whole mitt." "Naw I ain't seen that bitch since lunch time, she probably left after she ate. Whats up tho, whatchu niggaz doin down here?" I ask. "Danm shorty, what a nigga can only holla atchu on the block?" O responds. "Naw it ain't like that, Im jus sayin, I ain't expect ta see yall. I mean I ain't expect yall ta be....man light that blunt," I say after fumbling with an explanation to O's question.

"Scotty I see the bitches watchin shorty, go head you drive, imma hop in the back. Jus watch when you pullout, this mufucka got a mean take off, "O says as he's grabbing for the back door. "This mufuck got about ten drives, which one ta put it in?" I ask as I adjust the rearview mirror. "Jus put it in the first one, what's up tho is you ready or what? I know you goin ta school and shit so you not goin be able to play the morning shift but I got a special position for you to play if you wit it. Im bouta do something real big and im not going to be able to run back and forth as much as I use to. So this is where you come in at. I want you to hold the work down your spot and bring it up to Poka and them on a as needed bases. You not hot because the police don't see you as much, your house not hot so you don't have to worry about it gettin raided. You can move around without the police stopping and checking you, just keep a basketball in your hand or something to throw them off. Im going to pay you 500 a week, you goin to have the work in your house so if you want to hit the block and make somemore money you could. So what do you say, you down or what?" O asked looking me in my eyes thru the rearview. "Yeah im down," I said with a smirk and a nod of acknowledgment. "Thats what it is you bein down and all but turn this up, this my shit" Poka says as he turns up the car stereo and B.G's voice amplifies over the beat **I ducked off cuz the law lookin fa B.G/ sayin I killed a nigguh at the club last week** (We rode from my school back to the hood smoking and listening to Hotboyz Guerrilla Warfare.

"Yo, ride down Kareem bitch house," O says as we enter our neighbor- hood. "Which one? You know dat nigga swear he got all the bitches in the world" I respond. "The one that live by your grandmother, jus don't park in front the house, park a few spots back." "You wanna hit this blunt again Scotty?" Poka asked. "Naw im good," I say to Poka then ask O, "Am I good behind this van right here?" "Yeah, jus don't hit the curb and scrape my rims nigga." "How's that, am I too far out?" I ask. "Naw, you good, jus do me a favor; don't ever park so close behind another vehicle because we can't pull straight off. Sometimes a nigga ain't got time ta reverse an all that ol extra shit" O schooled me, "My bad im slippin." "It's cool thats what im here for, ta teach you niggas. Leave it runnin" O says as he exits the car and winks at me as if he jus read my mind.

O comes back to the car with a back pack hanging over his shoulders. "Yo drive up the wall" O says then asks Poka, "how much money you got on you off that shit?" "I got 7 from the G pack I finished last night and I probably made 5 this morning let me count it real quick. This $1,250 alltogether, imma give you the other buck fifty after I make a couple more sales," Poka says as he hands O a knot of money. "Where you want me ta park at?" I ask as we pull up to The Wall. "Jus pull up to the curb where Manna an Bean standin!" "You ugly as shit behind the wheel Scotty," Bean says as we pull up. I don't even respond I just break my mugg down and profile on em real slick. "Bean yall finished yet?" O asked. "Yeah a rush came thru this bitch, I finished and T-rod finished too, he told me to give you this money. He said he would be back tonight, him and Keyco went to handle something. I gave you two last night and this is the ova 5 to straightin that out, "Bean says as he hands O the money. "You finished too Manna?" O asked. "Naw, I got your money though. I still got a couple pills left but not enough too last me. Is it anymore shit out here?" Manna asked as he hands O money. "Naw thats the last of it, im bouta go grab up now tho" O says. "Ard we be out chere," Manna says.

"Scotty whatchu goin do? You gettin out up here or you want me drop you atcha house" O asked? "Run me to my house im goin to go eat an shit, then I be back up here," I say as I get out of the driver seat and into the passenger. "Aight rubberband this up for me real quick, a thousand in each rubber band no more than twenty ones then throw them in that bookbag." (I rubberband the money O had jus got from Manna an nem and threw it in the book bag not knowing it was already filled with rubber banded stacks of money. I played it cool tho and just looked at O with an approving nod then returned his wink from earlier as I got out of the car in front of my house.) "I be back in bout two hours, you goin be up there wit them niggas?" O asked me thru the rolled down car window. "Do I need to be," I asked really jus to hear O reaffirm my position? "Yeah I wanna holla at all of yall so if you see T-Rod let him know." "Ard" I say as i walk away from the car thinkin to myself *another speech*.

I stayed in the house for about an hour before I walked back up The Wall. I was suprised that none of my niggas was up there, just a fiend named Robo who lived in the building we hustled in front of. "Where da fuck erybody at Robo? What da police came up here?" I asked. "Naw soldier, they all in my house soldier: "Robo tells me with clenched teeth and popped eyes. You high as shit Robo ya mufuckin jaws is locked," I say laughing to myself then asking" who up there? "They all up there, Row came out here wit a big ass bag of weed. They all up there smokin in the backroom they might not hear the door so take my key soldier," Robo says handing me his key without ever un clinching his teeth. Then pops his eyes wider an says" tell Manna I got 14 left.

"Goddanm! It look like the fuckin room on fire, yall blowin it down in this bitch" I say as I shut the door behind me. "Yo what it is Scotty?" Row says. "We havin a domin party in this bitch; you roll it, you light it and you dome it. If you can't handle the heat 'choke choke' then get the fuck out da kitchen," he says then hands me a sandwhich bag full of weed.

"Yo shut up, this my part" Manna says half winning half leaning as he turns the volume up on the movie. "Beatrice ery month the mailman late wit my check, pass dem checks out on time." Man, smoke that nigga lil one." About an hour later the movie goes off! **Why you blockin us/balla blockin us/niggaz could keep tryin ain't no stoppin us** "Yo who the fuck is bangin on the door, "Bean yells. "Oh shit its probably Robo, he gave me his key," I say checking my pockets. "Im high as shit, I can't breath in this bitch!" Poka says leaving out letting Robo in. "Where is Manna at?" Robo asks. Here soldier im finished, I would have been up here but with the last pill I got me some head ha ha! You hear me soldier? I went and got my knob slobbed ha ha" Robo rants high off coke and drunk off cheap vodka. "Shut ya ugly ass up robo," Row says trying to spinkick Robo in his ass. "Fuck you Row you country ass nigga, you don't get no pussy anyway. Oh yeah, O rode past he said he down Vick house. Did yall save me the roaches? All that weed it should be some phat ones: phat as that freak!" "Shut the fuck up, you blowin my fuckin high," Lil Grezzy says cutting Robo off. "Come on, lets go holla at O," Manna says as he sparks his cigerette.

(Down vicks house, Vick is another fiend.)

"Yall niggaz high as shit, Row is ya eye's even open?" O asked.

"How much of that shit did yall smoke? All yall niggas stuck on stupid lookin like some fuckin zombies." O's brother kareem said. Yo im hungry as shit, let me hold the car right quick O ta run up the store?" I asked.

"Negative, you not drivin my car like that, you don't look like you can ride a bike right now. You betta tell Vick to walk up the store for you." "Ayyy Vick!!!" I yell up the steps, "bring ya frail ass down here and go up the store for me."

"All yall want somethin? Aight give me three dollars a piece, call yall order in and i'll go get it." Vick said.

"Hand me the phone Reem," I say..."yeah let me get a chicken filet on a bun with lettuce, tomatoes, mayonaise, salt, pepper, provolone cheese, regular cheese, bacon, lettuce and.. oh im high as shit did I already say ketchup? Well ketchup too and a order of onion rings and a White Grape Everfresh. Hold up, I got four more orders. What chall niggas want?" "Aight, aight, all right Miss, 15 minutes I be there. $36.50 I gotchu the name is Vick aight, you too. Yo Chinese people crazy as shit, here vick this ten. Get the rest from them niggas.

(Vick leaves to go to the store)

"Aight, now down to business." O said then began his speech, "Manna, you been hustling wit me the longest but i've been knowing all yall for a few years now and I grew ta look at chall like my family. Yall all know my brother, he was at the funeral when we lost Fezie. Look! I jus came from hollerin at my new connect, this nigga from Florida, he fucks wit me, he see im about that and I see yall about that so imma keep everything on the up an up wit yall. Yall not jus lil niggaz hittin packs for me, yall are family! Row what are you, 18? You what 17 Scotty? Manna I know ya lyin ass 15 about ta turn 16. So basically yall range from 16-18, the point im tryna make is that niggas out here yall age hustlin ain't doin it how we about ta be doin it. Them niggas might be yall friends, homeboys or whatever but we are family and family business is for family only. Im not sayin yall gotta cut niggaz off but they can only come so close because the closer a person is the more dangerous they become. I know yall niggas high so im not goin talk yall heads off. But what im tryna say is I just invested danm near everything I had into yall niggas because I beleive in yall niggas. Like I said yall family so I ain't keepin no secrets from yall. I had about $40,000 to my name after buyin this car an some other shit. I took $36,000 an bought 2 bricks from the connect for $18,000 a piece and he fronted me a 3rd brick. He said he would be back in a few weeks, I told em we could move a brick a week so he'll be back for his money and so we can copp again. The thing is this ain't the same coke we been sellin, they liked that other shit but they goin love this, this that fish, straight scale!" O said as he grabbed the backpack off the floor and dumped 3 bricks of fishcale cocaine on the table and said," look; this what we workin wit..3 bricks! Imma cook each brick and try to bring back a extra 12 ta 15 ounces off each joint, so we would have a little over 4 bricks of hard when i finish puttin a lil whip on it. I know yall use to me vialing the work up for yall but I feel yall would make out better if i jus gave it to yall by the ounce. The only thing is I don't want yall ta get petty an try to stretch it so much that the fiends don't wanna buy it. Every ounce I give yall I want back $950 and yall keep the rest but I want yall to only vial up between 15 to 17 hunnit off each ounce. That will still leave yall a nice profit. Scotty is gonna have the ouncs on deck for yall, so when yall done jus give him the $950 and he'll give you another ounce. Scotty imma smash you off every week but out of the 950 they give you for each ounce you keep $50 and put the $900 up for me. Is everybody cool with that?" O asked. We all simutanouslly said yeah. "Aight then, let's do this my niggas."

CHAPTER 5'S INTRO

At Vicks' house O cooked up one brick 36 ounce's. When he finished putting his whip game on it that 36 ounce's of cocaine was 49 ounces of crack. Not to mention all the extra grams he gave Vick. You know fiends judgement is normally bias, especially when your giving them free drugs but Vick insist the shit we got is a ten, better than what everybody else is selling so O broke it down ounce by ounce. 45 ounces individually wrapped, we chopped up four ounces into dimes since we were already at the table. Then O gave me 20 ounces he took the other 25 along with the two bricks of coke then we all did what it was we had to do. The next morning I must of had a weed hangover or I was just saying fuck school in my mind because my grandmother had to wake me up five times before I finally stayed awake.

CHAPTER 5
(HUSTLE&SCHOOL)

"What the fu...whatchu throw water on me for grandma?" I asked as I jumped outta my bed from the shock of the water just thrown into my face. "Cause im not walkin up these steps nomore, I figured that a get you up. I shouldn't have to wake you up no 5 times boy whats wrong with you," my grandmother said shaking her head as she walked out of my room. I took a quick shower, got dressed in some boot cut Gap jeans, a blue Nautica button up and some low cut all white Air Force Ones. (Its 2001, yeah I was wearing Gap, so what!} I put my Gap hoodie on under my Avirex leather that I got for Christmas. "Boy put a hat on" my grandmother yells as im trying to leave the house. After making a quick detour to find some early morning weed I got to school about 20 minutes late for second period. "Mr. Ray im glad you could make it" my teacher Ms. Fields says sarcastcally as im about to take a seat in the back of the class. "Better late than never, so i've heard anyway. "What I miss?" I say as I adjust my seat and sit my Everfresh Fruit Punch on my desk." Angie psssss Angie, give me some lotion im ashy as shit" I say with my book-bag covering my mouth as I take it off. "Ashey, more like high as shit, here boy," she says as she hands me the lotion. (As usual some ol square ass nigga don't know how to shut the fuck up and mind his business.)

"Sniff sniff somethin smell like weed," the square announces loudly from the middle of the class. "I should hit his bitch ass right in the head with this bottle," I whisper to Angie. But instead I handled the situation like an adult and said, "excuse me sir im trying to learn and I would appreciate it if you didn't make loud out bursts disturbing me and the rest of the class." Then focused my attention on Angie's open text book, trying not to make eye contact with Ms. Fields. But she's on to me and just shakes her head as if saying what am I going to do with this boy. The bell rings and the class starts to get up out of their chairs to exit the room. Im moving a little slow, my high is wearing down and I got the munchies, luckily its lunchtime. "Mr. Ray can i have a word with you?" Ms. Fields asked but I could tell it wasn't really a question.

(Aw man i don't feel like this shit right now. I gotta think fast excuse, excuse....) "But..but..its lunchtime Ms. Fields and I promised Angie I would treat her to lunch for helping me catch up and.."

"Mr.Ray we can chat now or at 3 o'clock, your choice but either way you owe me 20 minutes!" "Man, shit! "I say banging my hand on the desk in frustration, "sorry A, I hate to break a promise so here just treat one of your homegirls to lunch," I continue and hand her a ten and a couple ones out of my mitt which was only a little over two hundred dollars but it had to be atleast 60 ones so it looked like more.

"Thanks," Angie says then gives me a hug before she leaves the classroom. "Well, well aren't we mighty generous," Ms. Fields says, then continues, "I heard weed was the happy drug, I guess its true. What do you think Mr.Ray is it the weed or are you just generous by nature?"

"Its only lunch Ms. Fields, you act like I bought the girl a car or somethin," I respond.

"Well anyway, I would appreciate if you didn't come to my class late and high. I see something in you Mr. Ray, something special and if its brought out of you there's no telling how far you could go but your handicapping yourself with drugs and so on. Im not saying whether or not your a drug dealer, all im saying is i've seen how using and selling drug has effected so many people in a negative way. I to am from the projects and I had it just as hard as everyone else, yes I made some mistakes but I took control and guided my life in the right direction. I ...are you listening to me, why are you just staring at me like that?"

Danm Ms. Fields is sexy I say to myself, she looks like Jennifer Hudson after she lost the weight. "Oh im sorry, I just got so caught up in your words that I started to daydream about what you were saying." "Oh, and just what was i saying?"

"You were saying that if I apply myself I could be as special as a handicap person that took birth control and guided..."

"Mr. Ray you weren't listening to a word I said, its like my words are falling on deaf ears."

"Naw, im jus jokin I heard everything you said and I appreciate you taking your time to care. I don't know why I joke so much but seriously Ms. Fields can I go to lunch before its over, Im starving. "Im sure you are, your dismissed." "..Ay Ms. Fields before I go can I ask you something?" "Sure, whats on your mind?" "Well since Valentines Day is coming up and I wasn't sure what to get Angie, I didn't want to get her none of those cheap thoughtless gifts from the dollar store. I wanted to get her something nice." "Well im going to be getting out of here around four, if you hang around I could show you a nice place downtown." "Aight I guess its a date then," I say with a smile.

Ms. Field took me to a place called Godiva, its an expensive chocolate store. It was the perfect place to get a gift for my shorty and a few other people. I treated Ms. Fields to a crab cake from Phillips and then she dropped me off. You know I had to show off so instead of my house I got her to drop me off up The Wall. "Aigh't Ms. Fields, thanks" I say as im exiting the car. "All right," she replies, "but this doesn't look like your house to me."

"Yo who was that?" Manna asked as I approached him and T-rod.

"Oh, that's my teacher, she cool as shit."

"Gotdanm! She make a nigga wanna go back ta school, "T-rod says as he watches my teachers car turn the corner.

"What she took you shoppin? You got downtown locker room bags and what that say god..godi, what the fuck is that?" Manna asked.

"It's a chocolate store, she took me downtown ta grab some Valentines Day gifts. How that new coke doin tho?"

"Shorty it just slowed down, it was jammin all day up this bitch so I know its goin be mumpin tanight," Manna said feeling the bulges in his two front pockets for affirmation.

"You ready to go in the house ain't chu Scotty?" Tyrod asked then said, "here put some of this money up for me." Then hands me 1600 dollars, "here take this 19 hunnit and grab a ounce for me when you come back up. Matter fact can you vial it up for me?" Manna asked.

"Yo I can vial shit up in the middle of the night while my grandmother is sleep but til then ain't nuffin."

"Oh shit, here Scotty," Manna says holding out a pager then saying: "O gave me this for you he bought them for all of us. Everybody number is already stored in there."

"Ayyyye chic" I yell at my cousins car as she is riding past the block.

She stops and rolls down her window, "whats up Jamal?" She asked calling me by my birth name.

"Are you about to go down Granny's house?" I answer

"Yeah" she replies so I hop in the car with her putting my bags in the back seat of her Honda Accord and I tell my niggas "i'll be back."

CHAPTER 6 INTRO

Valentines Day fell on a Saturday and I was down my girl house nice and early. She was home alone because her mother's boyfriend took her mother to the Poconos and they aren't coming back til Monday. So I showed up at her house at about 11 that morning baring gifts; chocolates from Godiva, a stuffed teddy bear, a giant card, a pair of size 5 butter Timberlands and last but not least the magic stick. So my shorty comes to the door wearing white leggins, a lavender button up shirt from the GAP that falls right at her thighs, she has her shoulder length hair pulled back into a ponytail tied with a lavender something holding it in place with a pair of purple socks on. Now this might not sound sexy to yall but it was sexy to me.

CHAPTER 6
A VALENTINES DAY TO REMEMBER

"Aww, look at my chocolate cupcake lookin all sexy in her purple," I say half joking and half serious" Happy Valentines Day" I say as I hand Angie her gifts.

"Happy Valentines Day" she says back as we hug and kiss in the doorway then says, "ohh boy, get in here its freezing out there and I don't have no shoes on."

"Oh that's why ya nipple's hard, I thought you were turned on by my cute face," I say as I shut the door behind me.

"You know I love ya cute face," she says while pinning me to the door kissing me talking in between light pecks on the lips. "I wanna try something (kiss kiss) I read about in a magazine (kiss) your gift is upstairs," she says as she kisses me hard and pushes off of me then makes a run for the steps. (She on some cat an mouse shit I see) I let her get all the way up the steps before I grabbed her from behind and locked my arms around her flat stomach and lead her to the bedroom. "Do you like it?" She asked as we came thru the bedroom door. She got the red light bulb with the rose peddles on the floor the bed and a dresser full of utinsles: chocolate syrup, whip cream, ice, and scarf's. So im standing there in awe as my boo gets real seductive un-buttoning her shirt to reveal a pink lace..."strip," she says.

"You ain't gotta tell me twice, shit you ain't said nuffin butta word!" I say as I hastely began to pull my pants and shirt off. "Now lay down," she tells me. "Yo, ain't I suppos..." I began to object. "Ssshhh!" She sshhushes me and ties the scarf over my eyes and kisses my lips, then kisses my neck, then kisses from the top of my arm down to my wrist, lifting my arm up to the head board caressing my fingers then she began to tie my wrist to the headboard with another scarf. She repeats this procedure with my other arm. Kissing down my bicept to the the inside of my elbow, down my right forearm, kissing every letter on my R.I.P Fezie tattoo, then she ties that wrist also. Now I'm laying here wearing nothing but my Old Navy boxes and socks tied and blind-folded. A little nervous and a little excited at the same time, she must of had the CD on pause or something because I don't think the song starts like this but all of a sudden the room fills with music. (K-C and Jo-Jo) " All my life I prayed for someone like you, and I thank god, that I, that I finally found you!" As soon as I get relaxed with the music she starts to rub the corner of a half melted ice cub down my neck to my chest (no-homo) around my nipples, and every where she rubbed the cold ice she traced with her warm tongue. Licking up the drops of water the ice left behind, from my chest to my 6 pack or 4 pack she likes to call it stopping at my belly button. Then stripping me out of my boxers, where my soldier is standing at attention.

"Ooow!" I moaned lightly as she drops chocolate syrup on the head and shaft of my penis. Then licking swirls around the base of the head before taking half of me into her warm, wet, chocolate mouth. I guess chocolate does melt in your mouth and not in your hand. I was about to say, but before I could say anything she deep throats another inch or two of me and then guides her tongue back up my shaft to my head.

"Uhh... Uhh..." I was about to say something. Truthfully I don't know what I was about to say, I guess it doesn't matter because she shut me up again. Putting her index finger to my lips, Shusshing me again as she climbed on top of me. Clenching her hands under my chest to the outside of my six pack, seductivily working her hips to adjust me comfortably inside of her. In and out, up and down, left and right, leaning the upper half of her body onto the upper half of my body. Moaning and bitting my ear while still working her hips. I'm cumming she moans as she locks one of her arms around the back of my head and neck, then she locks the other arm around my back and the top of my shoulder. Burying her head into my neck bitting and moaning, this does it for me as I feel my lower body start to tingle. My back arches like im stretching or yawning as I grab the bars on the head board, it's like my mid section takes on a life of it's own. Grinding deep into her as I'm already deep into her. A noise exscapes her lips that I can't explain, as I shoot off into her, then I come back to earth.

The alarm clock on the dresser reads 5:21 p.m as I blink into focus. My arm is asleep with Angie asleep on it, so I try to manuever my body without waking her up, but between me wiggling from under her and the "beep beep beep beep beep beep," from my pager she awakes also. So I sit up, yawn, stretch, then shut off that damn beeping before I put my boxers on and go take a piss. I come back to the room to see that everyone with my number has paged me. I grab the cordless phone off the stand and call the last number that paged me which if I remember correctly is O, because his code is the number 0. "Man, what's up shorty? You aight? We was getting worried about you. Tyrod said you weren't at your grandmothers house and I drove Bean down your girls house, he said nobody ain't answer. We didn't know where else to look." O says through the phone. "Me and my girl was sleep," I tell O while im rubbing my free hand through Angie's hair. "Whats good though? Yall need me?" "Yeah, ain't nobody got nothing except Row, but them nigga's probably don't want no work right this minute cuz we all are about to go down Moe's and sit at the table with Jennifer, Jessica and them. Are you going or are you chilling?" O asked. "We aint leaving until about 7." "Alright, I'll be up there before then, where yall at?" "We all in Vick house, them niggaz smoking and drinking as usual and Row on the block. "Aight, tell them niggaz I will be up there." I say before I hang up with O. "So you leaving me? Huh punk?" Angie ask after I hung up the phone." "Just for a little while, I gotta take care of something but I will be back tonight around ten. You aint mad are you?" I asked. "Naw I aint mad, I did wanna spend the day with you though." Angie says. "Now you got me feeling bad. How about if I stop at Blockbuster and get a couple of movies on my way back?" I asked. "Just don't get nothing scary and your gift is in the closet," she tells me. "My gift, I thought you gave me my gift already?" I say as I reach in the closet and grab the Hects bag off the floor. "Wow this is nice, it must've cost you a nice peice" I say sizing up the white Tommy Hilfiger sweater up to my torso. "You got me the socks and boxers too, you went all out for me huh?" "It's just a lil something, something." She says imatating Martin Lawrence. "Did I tell you I love you today?" I asked. "Boy you are a mess," she says. "Yo, imma take a shower down here, matter of fact let me call O back and tell him to come pick me up in about a half hour. I'm not walking up that hill after I get out the shower."

"Do you want me to grab the money out of the house now?" I asked O on our way up Vick's house. "How much is it?" he asked. "Well, I rubber band them up into thousand dollar stacks and it's 8 of them. One got 11 hunnit in it." "So what you got 11 ounces left?" O asked. "Yeah, they sold eight of em, I sold one. I was on my way to school but it was so many sales lurking around out here I had to get that money. I aint even vial the ounce up, I just broke off pieces. All together I almost made fourteen hundred breaking off, I know some fiends got over but I wasn't mad, I made all that and still made it to school for lunch. Nigga I was in the line with about 15 hunnit on me, stuntin! I bought about ten bitch's Primetime Pizza." "Oh yeah, you did it like that shorty? Well go grab them stacks imma show you how to stunt nigga" O says. So I go in the house to grab the money for O and as soon as I get through the door I couldn't do nothing but laugh. My granny was having a card game, which was normal but the scene just caught me off gaurd. My grandmother was at the kitchen counter pouring some Bacardi dark rum into a glass, while one of her homegirls was at the table smoking a joint. Now I wasn't tripping off of that, it was my granny doing her two step while she poured her drink. She had my Tupac CD bumping as she sung along with the chorus.

And you Wonda why they call you bitch/ you wonda why they call you bitch, I betcha "Happy Valentines Day ladies," I say over the music and keep it moving upstairs to my room.

Back in the car with O I'm pulling stacks out of every pocket handing them to him. "Yo, where you said we going to Moe's?" I asked. "Yeah, we are treating Jennifer and her homegirls to dinner." On our way to Vick's house we ride past the block and holler at Row! "Yo, are you going with us or are you going to stay up here and hold it down?" O asked Row threw the car window. "Yo, it's jaming up this bitch, im not going no where. If yall not coming back tonight grab me two ounces Scotty! I probably pull an all nighter." "Aight, well we leaving in a minute, be careful out here! You don't get nobody to watch your back?" I ask him. "I'm good, I got Robo out here with me." "Aight, well imma run Scotty to grab them for you before we leave." "Aight, I'm here!" "Vick you ugly as shit," I tell him as me and O walk through the back door. "You look like the fucking Crypt Keeper ya skinny ass. Whats up my niggas?" I say to Manna, Bean and Polie. "I see yall got the slater girls up in here wit yall, Happy V-day ladies. Why the fuck ain't nobody put Vick on a leash before he bite one of them girls? At least put some paper down, he aint house trained yet." Everybody starts laughing as Vick cusses me out while he's walking out of the room. "God damn Jessica, what yall got a half of gallon of Hennessy? Yall doing it big, big drinks and big weed. I should of been came up here everybody got cups. Henny and cranberry, Henny and Sprite and Henny on ice. Where the cups at?" We kicked it for another 15 to 20 minutes then O asked if we were ready, Manna said he not driving in that county with his fucked up tags so he got in the car with O. So O and P drove, it was 9 of us in two cars. Five niggas and four bitches but we were not cramped.

At Moe's seafood restaurant we got two tables and started to order. "Oh my god this shit is expensive," Kelly says looking at the menu. "Just order what yall want" O says. "Don't worry about how much it cost, yall hanging with The Wall Boys tonight and this how we doing it."

"Well in that case..." Sherell says, "Let me get a lobster, I never had Lobster I've always wanted to try it." "Well for 56 dollars Rell, I can see why. I'll just taste yours" Jennifer says. "Imma order some Crab Imperial I had that before and it was good."

"Imma put yall on some good shit. The Chicken Breast stuffed with Crab meat, that's where it's at." I say bluffing like im a regular here. We ordered everything from Filet to stuffed rock fish to Seafood Alfredo you name it. With a couple pounds of Shrimp to nibble on while we waited for our main courses. So were at the tables drunk and high tripping waiting for our food.

"That's a cute sweater Scotty, Jennifer compliments. Where you get it from, Hects?" "Yeah, well it was a gift but it came from Hects. I'm trying not to waste Shrimp juice on it. Who wanna peel some Shrimp and feed em to me?" "This our day" Jessica interrupts, "If anybody should be getting fed Shrimp it should be me I mean Us!" "How is Valentine's days yall holiday? It's supposed to be a mutual thing, yall just took over this one huh?" O debates.

"I love Valentines Day, that's when yall bring out the sexy underwear you know the thongs and shit," Manna states. "All I wear is thongs," Sherell responds! "I don't wait for no fucking valentines Day for that!" "Girl I seen those granny panties hanging up on your clothes line stop lying!" Bean says joking. "Shut up boy, don't nobody wear no damn granny panties you probably be free balling nigga." Kelly says. "Come here, come check and see," Bean says smiling.

"If I wanted crabs I would have order them off the menu." Kelly says to Bean, we all laughed at the one.

$488.94 plus $48.89 was added as 10% gratuity which made the bill come to a total of $537.83. "What the fuck is gratuity?" Kelly asked. "I might be drunk but I aint that fucked up, I aint hear nobody order no fucking gratuity. "That's the tip, they add that to the bill to make sure the waiter gets their's too." O explains. "Where are we going to from here?" Jessica asks. Yall cool as shit I could chill with yall all night. "Well if yall want to, it's a Holiday Inn not to far from here. We could get a suite with the Jaquzzi and shit, we still got all that Henny in the car and I know yall niggas got some weed. No strings attatched or nothing, I dont want yall to think yall obligated to do nothing yall don't want to do we just chilling. Just look at it like a grown up sleep over and what ever happens, happens! I know I can keep a secret," O says. In the Holiday Inn parking lot O goes into the lobby to order the room while the rest of us are in the parking lot smoking cigerettes and talking shit to each other. My conscience is fucking with me because I promised my girl I was coming back but the Slater girls are all different shades of sexy. Red bones, carmel, brown skin, and we are all drunk headed to a hotel suite so the possibilities are endless. O comes swanking out of the front door of the hotel checking his pager, then goes to the pay phone at the side of the hotels entrance and calls a number out of his pager I assume because he's looking at his pager the whole time he is dialing. After a brief conversation he comes over to us with a concerned look on his face. "Yo, what's good?" everything aight?" we asked O. "Naw Row just got kidnapped!" He replies.

CHAPTER 7 INTRO

"O told P-olie to drop the Slater girls off and then meet us up Robo's. Me, Manna, and Bean rode to Robo's with O. On the way there O explained he got a page from a number he didnt know. The page had Row's code behind it with 911 behind that. When he called the number a bitch answered and she said they wanted $25,000 cash and a brick of coke. "When I get the money and the coke ready im supposed to page Row's pager with the code 25,000 behind my number and the kidnappers would give instruction on what to do with the money and drugs." When we got up The Wall O circled the block twice before we parked and got out. The block was like a ghost town it wasn't even any fiends lurking around, which is strange for a Saturday night. Robo lives in one of the apartments up The Wall. We went an banged on his door to see what he knew since Row said he was going to have him out there with him.

CHAPTER 7
A Valentines Day to remember!!!

"Who is it?" Robo yelled from the other side of the door. "It's O Robo open the door!" Robo opens the door holding a bloody wash cloth to the corner of his forehead. "They got Row, those bitch ass niggas got one of our soldiers O," Robo cries (not literally)!

"Slow down Robo, who got Row? Just tell us what happened!" O instructed. "It was jammin up here O, money was coming from everywhere, Row got tired of keep running back and forth to the stash so he was keeping like 50 pills on him at a time and I was at the top of the steps watching the street. So the police wouldn't run down on my lil soldier. Row had like 10 sales lined up serving em out of his hoody, and im just glancing back and forth from the street to Row but im mostly watching the street until I heard Row say "What the fuck!" I looked and seen a nigga had him pressed up against the side of the building so I jumped down the steps and ran over there that's when some nigga, not the same nigga that was holding Row, another nigga smacked me a cross my head with a big ass gun. I fell down on one knee and I seen the nigga who had Row jacked up was strapped too and he was putting handcuffs on row. So I thought the police had snuck in the line disguised as sales, but they wasn't no fucking police cuz they threw Row in a van. You know the kind with the door on the side that slide, it was one of them. The niggas aint get out of that van tho, cuz I seen when the van pulled up it was a bitch in there and she was by herself. She had a fitted hat on, but anyway they took Row to the van and threw him in it and pulled off." Robo said. "Who was the nigga Robo,

What color was the van?" O asked. "I aint get a good look at their faces, the nigga that had Row had his back to me and the nigga that smacked me with the gun I wasn't really paying him no attention. I was focused on Row, plus it's so dark down here since yall shot all the street lights out. One of the niggas had dread locks cuz I seen them hanging out his hat he had on one of them dollar hats, the wool ones, what yall call em, oat meals? Both of the niggas had on black oatmeals and black hoodies. I think the Van was black or it could of been dark green or dark blue it was dark colored. I aint pay the van no mind at first, I was looking at the bitch in there I know she had glasses on. Because I was saying why is this bitch driving at 11 oclock at night with shades on."

(Bang, Bang, Bang, Bang) "Open the door," P-olie yells from outside.

"Why the fuck is he banging on the door like he the police" Robo says unlocking the door.

P comes in and he got Lil Greezy, Poka, and Ty-rod with him. Lil Greezy comes straight in and slides his sawed off shot gun out of his sleeve like he is on a movie or something catching it by the handle. I think he just sit in the house practicing that move. Tyrod goes in his waist and pulls out a 13 shot high point 9mm.

"I got this from Keyco, he wasn't trying to give me his 40 cal, but I can work with this" Tyrod says.

"I got my 38 uptown and Big Greezy got my 357" Manna says.

"Ask Keyco do he got some extra shells for that 9 Tyrod cuz my man around Hillside told me if I get some shells I could come and get his 9," Bean said.

"I got a whole box of of shells in P car, Keyco gave me a extra clip and all that. I'm ready, just point a nigga out! Who got Row? Yall aint heard nothing yet?" Tyrod says while clicking his guns safety on and off.

"Naw O answered, but you know the streets talk, you said it was about 10 fiends in line, maybe one of them got a good look at one of the niggas. Scotty you and Poka don't have no joints (guns), I got a 380 and a 25 I will bring out here tomorrow just give me a minute to think. Imma figure something out. We dont even have $25,000 to give these niggas, then the connect will be here in about 2 weeks. Look let me

make a few calls, sit down and think for a minute imma figure something out. Until then keep yall eyes and ears open. Niggas caught us
with our gaurd down, T-rod watch me to my car. We cant get caught
slipping no more it's war now, imma bring them guns out here for yall
tomorrow Scotty and Poka. All yall good? Don't nobody need me to
drop them off no where? Well alright, I love yall niggas. I see yall in the
morning," O said as he left out the door with Tyrod trailing him with
his gun in his hand.

"Yo what the fuck happened to your head Robo?" Poka asked as he
was lighting a blunt off of the stove.

"The whores shorty! The whores smacked me with the gun when they
grabbed Row.

"Where the fuck yall was at Poka?" I asked unaccussingly.

Tyrod had me and Lil Greezy over some bitches house that live around
the corner from him. "Scotty them bitches was bullshit thinking they going smoke all my weed up they had another thing coming. We was over
Keyco house playing Madden for money when P paged us though, I heard
yall was stuntin out wit the slater girls, eating Lobster and Shrimps and
shit. Yo, you think them bitches had something to do with it?"

"Do with what?"

"With Row getting snatched."

"Naw, I doubt it." I said.

"What about the VA boys? You think it was them niggas? You know
"Sim" (Seam) just came home. I dont know Robo did say one of the niggas
had dreads and alot of them VA niggas got dreads. We could go over there
and buy some grass and see if they act different or they might of heard
something." I say.

I knew Sim since the seventh grade. If he heard something he might
tell me.

"Come on lets go over there, then we can go around Hillside and get
that joint from my man" Bean says jumping out the chair.

"We don't need to ride that deep, so all of us don't have to go" P says.
"Scotty go get the joint from T-rod." "Bean, Lil Greezy and I are going
to ride over there.

Just then T-rod comes back in Robo's, I get the gun from him then we ride over to the VA boys strip to buy some weed and see if we can find out any thing. Their strip was mostly apartment complexes like ours, but it was some project row houses scattered around the apartments.

"It don't look like nobody out here." P says.

"Pull over right here we going to go in the buiding," I tell P. "The weed house is on the 2nd floor keep it running P we will be right back."

Me, Bean, and Lil Greezy go to the buiding. It's locked, their buidings are the same as ours if the door shuts it locks on the outside. So we normally keep a rock, a chair or something to stop it from shutting all the way. Bean bangs on the door and quickly someone yells from the inside.

"Who is it!"

"It's Bean!"

"What Bean?"

"String Bean, from The Wall!"

(There's a little whispering inside, then the door opens)

Inside the building it's about 20 niggas 8 bitches a couple 5ths of liquor and blunts being passed around, 2 crackheads waiting to be served and I can only imagine how many guns are on deck in the multitude of niggas, but I don't know all this yet.

"Whats up, shorty got some weed on the second floor?" I asked.

"Yeah she straight, just knock on the door.

As we get half way up the steps thats when we see how deep it is in the building. It's alot of different emotion in the buiding. Some of the VA boys straight up don't like us for whatever reason and some of them fuck with us. The shit crazy for real because no matter what strip or set you claim, Up The Hill, Down The Hill, Coppin Court, Hillside, The Wall or VA (you'll learn more about the other strips later down the road) all of us grew up together. We all went to the same middle schools together, we all played on the same teams. I dont know if it was the few blocks of seperation or what, but something lead to us all hating each other and the hood would eventually become a war zone, but right now is the early years and the fire is just starting to get hot. So where was I? Oh yeah the 2nd floor, "Whats up Loc dog?" I say as I reach the 2nd floor.

"Whats it is Scotty boy?" he says back. "What you don't fuck with a nigga since I ain't down the school no more?"

"Come on Loc, you know you my nigga, if you don't get no bigger." I tell him.

"You know Sim home" he says.

"Yeah I heard they none processed his attempt, where that nigga at?" I asked Loc.

"In the weed house probably trying to get his nuts out the sand. Imma tell em you out here!" "Here Loc, grab this weed for me since you ready to go in there see if she will give me 6 for fifty.

(Loc walks in the house, Bean is on the step, talking to a couple of niggas. I can't hear what they are saying but their body language is telling me everythings cool. Lil Greezy is standing with his back against the wall looking like he's ready to drop that shotgun out of his sleeve at the drop ash).

"Scotty whats up shorty?" Sim says stepping out the door in sweatpants and a tanktop. We slap hands and pull each other in to a man hug where I have to position myself so my waist doesn't get to close and the metal doesn't make contact with him alarming him or making him think im on some bullshit.

"What's up Bean, Lil Greezy?" Sim says being courteous while im grabbing the weed from Loc dog.

"Whats up Sim" Bean and Lil Greezy speak back.

"I seen Big Sexy and Lil Glenn over the jail, Sexy said the police on his case he is under investigation for planting evidence so he might be ready to get his case thrown out and they dropped Lil Glenn gun charge he was putting in for a bail review to get a bail for the drug case." Sim told me.

"Yo, you aint see Big Wall?" I asked sim.

"Naw, I heard he was on lock-up for throwing piss on somebody or something like that."

(HONK! HONK! HONKKK!)

"Damn, I almost forgot P was out there." I say as I slap hands with Sim and Loc-dog, "yo come over the wall and holla at me when you get a chance," I say as we head back to the car.

"Yo what the fuck took yall so long?" P said when we got back in the car.

"That wasnt even no long time" I say, "dont start that bullshit P."

"Yo, ride around Hillside P, Im trying to grab that joint asap" Bean said.

"What them niggas say? Do you think they got him?" P asked.

"I cant really say."

We pulled up in the parking lot down Hillside. I dont feel like getting out the car, these Bean homeboys it aint like over VA where its a bunch of mixed emotion, no snake shit or none of that. I aint going to lie I like how they carry it down here, alot like us their click grew up together around each other and they stick together. Some clicks got clicks inside of a click and thats just trouble waiting to happen. So Bean gets out by his self I recline my seat all the way back and put the 9mm on my lap.

"Yo, you think they might torture Row or do some sick shit like in the movies?" I say to nobody in particular.

"I dont know, do you think O going to pay the ransom?" P asked.

"He got to, what choice do we have" I say back to P.

"But if Row know who kidnapped him, they probably get the ransom money and still kill him."

"All I know is when we find out who got Row imma take em down the woods and put this pump in they mouth and blow the whole back of their head off, Click Clack.

"Yo stop playing wth that fucking gun behind me Lil Greezy." P says.

"Man this my baby right here, she aint going to do nothing I dont tell her to do." Lil Greezy says while rubbing the barrel of his pump.

"You ever killed a nigga before?" I asked Lil greezy.

"Naw" he replies, but I seen my brother smoke a nigga and I wanna see how that shit feel.

"I shot at some niggaz" I say "Me and T-rod was robbing them and the niggas tried to run I dont know if I shot the niggas or not, but I dont feel no different. What about you P? You eva kill or shot a nigga?

"This one time my girl was somewhere she aint have no business being for real but she was with her homegirl and whatever happened my girl wouldnt talk to the other niggas or some shit like that and they beat my bitch up. O took me up there I shot the whole porch up, we watched that shit on the news. 3 niggas got hit but aint nobody die.

"Scotty! Bean says as he taps the window. "Give man one of those bags of grass."

I rolled down the window and gave the bag of weed to Bean, he gives it to the nigga standing next to him, they slap hands and bean gets back in the car.

"Lift ya fucking seat up Scotty, you all sleep with the joint in ya lap." Bean says.

"I wasnt sleep nigga, I was thinking did you get the joint?"

"Yeah bitch pretty too."

"Let me see it, ooh this nice"

"The bullets in the glove box" P says.

"Yo, run down the gas station so we can get some Dutch's," I tell P. "We might as well crash at Robo's it's damn near one o'clock I know my girl mad and sleep, I aint about to go down there. Shit Valentines day over with anyway," I say.

"Yeah this one to remember right here," P says as he turns out of hillside parking lot.

CHAPTER 8 INTRO

We went back to Robo's and smoked until we passed out. I woke up the next morning around 11 with a cramp in my neck from sleeping on that couch. I grabbed a half smoked blunt out of the ash tray and lit it with a lighter that was on the end table with all the rest of the contraband weed, guns, bullets ect. I guess the smell of weed just has that effect on pot heads because as soon as I blew out that first cloud of smoke mufucka's start shifting around on the couch waking up.

CHAPTER 8

"What time it is Scotty?" Poka asked me while he was yawning and stretching.

"It's two of" I say in response as I fake a glance at my watch.

"Two of what?"

"Two of these muthafucking nuts!"

"Man fuck you see me over on that blunt." Poka says getting up to go to the bathroom.

I hit the blunt and observed the room. You got Manna on the love seat he got his Rockports on the floor next to his pack of cigarettes his feet are proped up and crossed on the coffee table with his hand in his pants like Al-Bundy. Lil Greezy sharing the love seat with him had his back to Manna half curled in the fetal position. He still has on his black wool hat (oatmeal), with that damn pump leaned up against the side of the chair. Bean in the recliner he got the chair reclined almost as flat as a bed and he's curled up on his side. The two's 9mm are on the coffee table with an unrolled bag of weed about 8 half drunken beverages an empty 9mm clip and a box of bullets. T-rod and P are sleep in Robo's guest bedroom I expect since P car keys are on the table and T-rod 9 still here.

"Let me hit that Scotty" Poka say coming back in the living room.

"Yo, this year is just starting and we lost Fezie and now I dont know how this Row shit going to turn out." I say as I hand Poka the blunt.

BEEP! BEEP! BEEP! Beep!

"That aint me" I say grabbing my pager checking it to make sure.

"That's my shit" Poka says grabbing his beeper from out the crease of the couch. "This O hand me the phone Scotty."

I hand him the phone and he hands me the blunt.

"Yall ugly as shit, doming the weed throw me my soda Scotty" Bean says as he wakes up.

"Which one is yours?"

"The Fruit Works, the orange one."

"O said he on his way out here" Poka tells us as he hangs up the phone.

"What else he say?" I ask Poka.

"Shit, told me tell yall dont go nowhere"

"Yall should of told em bring us breakfast."

"Ay Robo, go up the store for us" Bean yells from the living room to Robo's bedroom.

"Yo what the fuck we doing today? It dont seem right hustling like everything is everythin and Row somewhere getting tortured and shit" I say.

Manna wakes up and lights a cigarette and that triggers Lil Greezy.

"That fucking cigarette stink Manna" Lil Greezy says reaching for his Everfresh Apple Juice.

"Who said go up the store?" Robo asked coming out of his bedroom. "I need me a shot of Black Watch anyway. Aw man its sunday the Liquor Store or the Carry Out not open.

"Imma drive across the tracks" P says coming out of the back room. "What time is it? Is Mcdonalds still serving breakfast?

"I got two of" Poka says to P.

"Two of what?"

"Two of theeeeeeeese nuts did you get em?" Poka says as him and I bust out laughing.

"You with that shit too Scotty?" P ask. "Both of yall whore's going starve, who riding with me across the tracks?"

Robo jumps up! Im going soldier fuck Poka and Scotty country asses.

"Shut the fuck up Robo, before a nigga split the other side of your head." Poka tells him.

"Aye yo fuck you soldier, that's a war womb" Robo says touching his scar.

"Im going too" Lil Greezy sayd to P, "Imma leave my baby here but imma take this just to be on the safe side." Lil greezy says grabbing Bean's chrome 9 off the table.

(Robo, Lil Greezy and P-olie leave to go get food!)

"Yo that's all we got is this one bag of weed left?" Tyrod ask walking into the living room grabbing it off the table. "Who got dutches?"

"The dutches on the sofa an I got anotha bag of grass round here sumwhere," Poka tells Tyrod.

I get on the phone and call Angie.

"I can't fuckin beleive you, the one day out the year for us and you leave me in the house by my fuckin self!!! You don't call and let me know you okay or nuffin, do you know I called the jail, the hospital, I even called ya grandmother. That lady had no idea where you were that was so inconsiderate of you."

Whole up yo! You think I ain't wanna call or be with you? Somethin came up, I can't really say what it is but yo im still not in my right frame of mind i'll make it up to you I just need you to bare with me for a minute." I made my plea with Angie thru the phone.

It took me almost an hour of smoothing her over before I could tell I was really back in her good graces.

"Aight I love you too baby, everything will be back to normal in a few days I promise," i say before hanging up the phone.

"I love you too, I promise baby.."Poka adds laughing with Manna.

"Sssh! Yall hear that," Tyrod says grabbing the 9 off the table and Manna grabs the pump, they both put their ears to the door.

"Shut da fuck up! Get up there!" We hear someone's hushed voices say in the hall.

"Open the door," Manna says to me inadaublely. I do and they turn the corner of the door frame Manna going low with the pump and Tyrod going high with the handgun. I ain't goin lie that shit looked slick.

"Watch out let em in," Tyrod says as P-olie, Lil Greezy and Robo man handle a fiend thru the door of Robo's apartment.

"Lock the door," Lil Greezy says as he pushes the fiend onto Robo's couch pointing the gun at his chest.

"Shorty, what I do shorty?" The fiend ask damn near in tears.

"Shut the fuck up we askin the questions here," Lil Greezy tells the fiend.

"You came up The Wall and copped lastnight?" P asked agressively.

"Aww man, I knew I shoulda went ova VA and copped" the fiend whined.

"Jus answer the fuckin question," Manna yelled while raising the pump to the fiends head.

"Ye, Ye, Ye..Yeah I copped up here lastnight," the fiend stuttered.

"Who was the niggas in line that grabbed the nigga that was hittin?"

"Shorty I don't know nobody, I mind my.."

"Man smoke this nigga, he think a nigga playin wit his bitch ass we goin smoke him and ery ova fiend that was in that line if they don't tell us what we wanna know. Robo turn the radio up as loud as it go," Lil Greezy says.

"Aight soldier" Robo says as he goes to turn on the radio.

(knock, knock, knock!)..(knock!knock!knock!) Its me yo, open the door" O says from the other side of the door.

Bean lets O in the apartment.

"Who da fuck is dis nigga?" O says twisting his face up.

"He about ta be John Doe when I blow his fuckin head off because ain't nobody goin be able ta reconize em. Turn that radio up again, in't shit change" Manna says.

"Whoe, whole on Robo, look main man I don't know you an I don't wanna see you get smoked for nuffin. You was in line wit them niggaz I know you heard em talkin or something," I say to the fiend.

DANGA!!! It's been so long/you've been gone/get on da floo for the nigga right chere, sing it..DANGA!! Mystikal's song Danger blast thru the radio at max volume.

"Wait..Wait..Wait..I swear..." the fiend attempts to plead.

"Uh-un," Manna says shaking his head from left to right while raising the shotgun to the man's face again.

"HOLD," I say pushing the barrel of the shotgun down with my left hand and signaling for Robo to turn the music down with my right.

"Wat da fuck is you doin Scotty," Manna said with murda in his eyes.

"Wait what unk? You betta tells us summin for he push ya shit back, this ya last chance I can't save you after this." I inform the fiend.

"Aight..Aight umm jus let me think a minute," the fiend says.

"Don't think about lyin either cuz if what you say don't add up to what we already know.."Lil Greezy warns him.

"Aight please don't kill me shorty this all I heard one of the nigaas say, I was danm near last in line. It was only about two people behind me and I think they were together. When I notice one of the guys in front of me ease out of the line but he didn't ease to the front he ease'd to the back behind the last two people and im thinking to myself thats strange cuz as good as those black tops is who the fuck move to the back of the line runnin the risk of yall sellin out or whatever. Anyway when he walked past me the other nigga took a step to follow him and I heard him say ONE-EYE where the fu..like he was about to ask him where he was going then caught hisself but I definitely heard the name One-Eye but thats all I heard I copped and got outta there." The fiend told us.

Manna and O looked at each other like they were reading each others minds or at least thinking the same thing.

"Let that Man up" O said. "This shit never happened aight" O warns the fiend.

"Aight" the man obliged.

"Aye come back up here when we open the shop up, imma do something nice for you, you hear me." O tells the fiend walking him to the door.

"Yo, where the fuck yall find yo at?" O asked as he takes a seat on the couch. "Oh shit" he says taking the 380 and the 25 out of his pockets as he leans up and then sits back down. Robo spotted that nigga when we was coming from across the tracks we followed him for a lil while then threw his ass in the trunk.

"You think that fiend going to send the police up here?" I ask.

"Naw, that's why I told him imma do something nice for him, they love this coke they'll sell their soul for it. I can't believe yo said it was the nigga ONE EYE, well I can believe it. I would have never thought to guess his bitch ass but I can believe it."

"Aight, now we know who got him, what we going do to get him back? I asked.

CHAPTER 9'S INTRO

The plan was simple, we was to discretly follow this nigga ONE EYE hopefully he would lead us to Row, but if the oppurtinity presented it self we would throw ONE EYE in the trunk take him somewhere, then torture him until he told us where Row was at. O drove his car home and came back in a car I never seen before then him and P went and rented a station wagon. O's brother Kareem spent most of the day with us teaching us the in's and outs of how to murder a nigga. He got one of his bitches cars and we took turns riding around with him looking for the nigga ONE EYE. At about 6:30 or so it was starting to get dark and we caught a break. It was me, Reem, and Manna riding together. Manna had went home earlier and got his 38, Reem had T-Rods 9 because T-Rod was up Robo's chilling. We were taking turns looking for ONE EYE and I had the 380, when Manna says ride past Bethune because he needed some weed.

CHAPTER 9
(The Simple Plan)

"Hol, hold, naw Reem keep going don't stop right here. Yall aint see that?" Manna asked.

"See what? You geeking shorty why would you tell me to hold, don't stop. Hold mean stop, so you just told me to stop, don't stop.

"My bad Reem but I just saw that nigga he walked around the building," Manna said excitedly. "You aint see him Scotty?"

"Who ONE EYE?" I asked.

"No, Tupac! Yeah ONE EYE who the fuck else imma be talking about? Park by the dumpster Reem, come on Scotty we going meet his ass around this end. Put them masks on now don't wait until yall get round there and Scotty cock one in the chamber now!" Reem tells us. Me and Manna run to the oppossite side of the building hoping to meet the nigga and catch him by suprise, so we lean up against the building and Manna peeps around the corner. "Where he at?" I whisper.

"He still on the other end, I think he going go back the way he came."

"Let me see" I say. I look and see the nigga, he's mostly facing the street with his hands in his hoody. "What you wanna do? We probably can get halfway down on em before he see us then he aint going have the time to run."

Manna cocks the hammer on his 38 and says come on. We spin the corner and take about six steps with our guns in hand. That's when the nigga looks then does a double take and takes a step back like he is about to take off running but without even taking his hand out of his hoody.

"Blogup! Blogup!" "BAP! Bap! Bap!" "Boom! Boom! Boom!" We exchange shots, with ONE EYE taking a giant step back towards the corner with every shot he lets off. "BLAGUP!" His last shot before he turns the corner knocking feathers out of my Triple Fat Goose coat right around my under arm.

Manna looks at me and then my coat then I lift my arm up and feel the area.

"Ah shit, that bitch shot me!" I say as I lightly touch my finger against the spot I feel burning.

"Come on Manna says as we run back around the corner the way we came. Once we cut across the second set of houses we see Reem standing out of the car with his mask on aiming the 9 with both hands.

FLOP! FLOP! FLOP! FLOP! FLOP! FLOP! FLOP! Reem unloads as we get closer to Reem we see ONE EYE grab his left thigh and reaches his right hand over his shoulder and shoots two blind shots. Blagup! Blagup! Before turning the corner.

"What the fuck happened?" T rod asked as I come through Robo's door with my coat in my hand and the long john thermal shirt im wearing is stained with blood under the arm.

"Let me see that shit again Scotty, I couldn't really see in the car" Manna says as im lifting my long john shirt over my head.

" It aint that bad it just grazed you under your under arm. You probably dont even need stiches"

"Yo what the fuck happened?" t rod yells getting irrated we are ignoring him.

"We just shot out with that bitch on the weed strip." I say.

"Did yall kill him?"

"Naw, I dont think so anyway I know he got hit. I think it was just in the leg though, give me a cigarette Manna, we need some weed. Where the fuck is everybody at anyway?" I asked.

"P-Olie and Poka out lerking. O, Bean, and Lil Greezy together. Where is Reem at with my joint?"

"He be back he went to go switch cars, yo page everybody so we can all be on the same page" Manna says.

About an hour later the whole team is back up The Wall in Robo's apartment.

"Aw, man you ight nigga, you aint get shot you got skinned. Yall had to see this nigga him and Manna run back to the car Scotty dives across the back seat like he about to pass out or some shit like that. How the fuck you managed to get shot anyway? "Yall creep a nigga and"... "I aint see the shit coming.

The nigga never whipped out he shot striaght through his hoody I aint going lie I wasn't expecting that."

"He sized us up when he took that first step back" Manna says.

"Yeah I thought he was ready to run, thats why when he started shooting I could'nt really aim I just shot in his direction" I say.

"Well you see what happened when I lined him up between these scopes" Reem brags.

"Yeah I seen him grab his leg" I say. "And that was from a block away after I heard yall shots I seen him come around the building I thought he was going to run right into me, but he ran across the street instead of down to me" Reem says.

"I was going to chase the nigga, but I aint know how bad Scotty was hit, so we just ran back to the car" Manna says.

"I aint know how bad I was hit I felt the sting but I was waiting for the rest of the pain, I mean I felt it but im like is this it?"

"Ha ha, my nigga a soldier! Is this it? You heard what the fuck he said give me some love soldier!" Robo says drunk as shit off of black watch.

"Yo they probably really ready to let Row have it now" Poka says.

"I dont know aint nobody see yall faces, he dont know who was shooting at him!" O says then tells us, "I hollered at some people around the hood so soon as he shows his face we going to know".

(Knock knock knock)

"Who is it?" Robo yell drunkly.

"It's Row!"

"Row" we all whispered to ourselves, click click we start cocking our guns.

"A nigga feel like playing huh" Reem says moving to the side of the door. "Open the damn door!"

"Open it Robo," O says while we got about seven guns aimed at the door.

First ONE EYE and _____ try to kill me, then I come up here and yall got a hunnit guns pointed at me" Row says and then smiles and walks in the door.

"Lock that door Robo" O says as we all show Row love like he just hit the winning shot in the championship game.

"What they let you go?" "You aight?" "Did they feed you?" "Did they torture you?" "How you get here?" "Where they had you at?" We all threw questions at Row before he could even sit down.

"Whoaa let me sit down shit, where the weed at?" Row says touching the cuts on his forehead. "That shit stop bleeding?" he asked no one in particular.

"What the fuck, they work you over in there then let you go?" P joked then got serious. "Naw all jokes aside how you get back?"

"Man these bitch ass niggas left some bitch watching me, this bitch wanna keep trying to hold on a coversation with me so I said aight bitch you wanna be so friendly take these cuffs off me so I can take a shit. So she took the cuffs off me, the whole time she had a tre pound or a thirty eight pointed at me I was ready to try and rush the bitch and take it from her but I seen I could just dive throught the bathrrom window I knew the bitch would only have enough time to get one shot off. That bitch took it too. I don't know what she hit, but it wasn't me thank GOD. Once I hit that ground outside all I could think was two words, Im gone."

"Where the fuck they was holding you at?"

"Out brooklyn, I walked out here hitting the dope stroke the whole way up this bitch. Wait til I see One Eye, imma air his bitch ass out him and _____ I probably blow that bitch too. Yo im trying get high, take me to get some weed P."

"You know niggas caught One Eye down Bethune on the weed strip a couple hours ago. Manna and Scotty ran down on him Scotty got grazed in the ribs, Reem caught yo trying to get away!"

"Hell no, For real?" Row says.

"Show him Scotty!"

I lift my long john shirt up and show Row, "yeah that bitch was strapped" I tell row.

"Man we got to get some weed come on P" Row says and grabs the 380 off the table.

"Its only 6 shells left in there" I tell Row so Tyrod grabs his 9 an says he got a fresh 13, Row's good and they leave Tyrod, P, and Row.

"Yall niggas aint had shop open all day? Im going across the street to get me two of them gold tops they aint no blacks but they aight Robo says and leaves out to go cop.

BEEP! BEEP! BEEP!

"Oh shit, this yo!" O says "ride with me right fast Reem and Manna!" O gets on the house phone for a minute then him Manna, and Reem leave and their all strapped.

Me, Poka, Lil Greezy, and Bean stayed in Robo's waiting for the others to get back.

"Yo how long it take niggas to go cop some weed? God damn!"

"Yeah them niggas have been gone for a minute, Robo aint even come back yet."

"Sssh, yall hear that?"

"Yeah it sound like they shooting down the hill!"

5 minutes later P-olie, Row, and T-Rod come back in Robo's.

1 2 3 4 5 6 7 damn seven police cars just went down that bitch Row says while he's peeping out the window.

Tyrod throws 8 bags of weed and two boxes of Dutch's on the coffee table.

"Yo somebody call the pizza joint, I aint going back outside tonight. I kow the police going to be buzzin pulling everything over." Polie says.

"What happened out there?" I ask as Im reaching for the phone.

RIIINNNG RINGG it starts ringing as soon as im about to grab it!

"Whoa now, who this?" I answered the phone, "it's me scotty O tells me through the phone. I just wanted to let yall know we good, we aint coming back up there tonight just tell everybody I love em and we going hook up tomorrow." "Aight thats what it is. We love you too nigga," I tell em before I hang up.

A couple minutes later Robo walks through the door and says "it's hot as shit out there police everywhere somebody just got smoked."

CHAPTER 10'S INTRO

Come to find out when we shot on Bethune (the weed strip) and the nigga One Eye grabbed his leg and let off the two blind shots he got hit but it was only a flesh wound. The nigga tied a scarf around his leg and went around braggin like he was Rambo or some fucking body but a couple of hours after the shoot out on Bethune a couple niggas with mask on ran down on him, I guess his luck ran out cuz he aint even make it to the abulance. When the cops got there he was pronounced D.O.A (Dead on Arrival)! Oh well, better him than me! I didnt get in the house that night til damn near one in the morning, only to argue another half an hour with my grandmother for waking her up. I argued that I needed a key and she said I wasn't getting another one since I lost the last two. And when I say argue I don't mean that literally because I don't cuss or fuss at my granny. I only can remember one time I raised my voice at her so when I say argue, I really mean debate. Anyway I couldn't sleep when I got in so I took a quick shower then chopped up coke in the bathroom with the shower water running so if my granny was still woke she wouldn't hear the razor keep hitting the plate. I went to sleep at about 4AM and granny woke me up at seven. I didn't fall back to sleep or nothing, I might of been excited to get to school to give Miss. Fields her gift I had gotten a bunch of Valentine's Day hearts for different people. Angie, Angie's mother, my granny, Miss. Fields, and so on and so on. So I left my first period which was Shop Class (Carpentry) about five minutes early so I could beat the rest of the class to Miss. Fields room and give her the gift with out being on blast.

CHAPTER 10
Call it Even

Everyone take a seat, I know you all missed me but lets simmer down Miss. Fields announces to the class.

"Oh my god your in class on time, let me check your temperture." Angie says putting her hand on my forehead.

"I know right, look at me showing off" I say. "If you want I could have my Hack pick you up in the morning and we could ride to school together."

"Boy you come to school on time once a month and now your going to start picking me up? Yeah right, oh and you need to start calling me and letting me know your in the house because I heard all those shots last night and I was worried. And why don't I have your pager number, whats up with that?" "Does anybody wanna share their weekend? Since I see everyone having private discussions, does anyone want to share with the class?" Miss. Fields announces.

"Oh let me tell the class about what you did to me this weekend, girl you deserve a trophy or something!" I say playfully to Angie.

"Go ahead tell em, and I bet I'll never do that shit again blabber mouth."

"Im just fucking with you A, you know what happens in your room stays in your room."

I felt my pager vibrating so I checked the number and seen that it was O. I knew I should have bought that work to school with me but me being the smart nigga I am. I know how to improvise. "Psss, pssss, aye pass this note to Foolish for me," I tell the nigga sitting behind me.

Foolish grabs the note and reads it then gives me the thumbs up, after he stuffs the ten dollars in his pocket. "Miss fields can I go to the bathroom?" Foolish asks.

"Sure your excused" Miss fields tells him. About five minutes later (DING DING DING) "Class everyone single file line through the door and towards the exit, this is a fire drill." While the whole schools outside for the fire drill im on the pay phone in front of our school calling O.

"Whats up? You in school shorty?" O asked.

"Yeah I knew you were going to page me I need to start listening to my first instinct. Something said bring that shit with me, fuck it just come down here and get me if you can make it in the next half hour or so I should be out here in the parking lot. If not just page me from the pay phone on the side of the school and i'll be out there.

About 15 minutes later I saw O's Acura slow rolling into the parking lot, I Iift my arms up to get his attention. He pulls up on me and Angie and a few others, "I know you Love that hot boy shit shorty but what you set the school on fire?" O ask through the window then laughed a corny laugh at his own joke. "Something like that" I reply with a half smile.

"Why didn't you wear a jacket out here A?" I ask while im unzipping my hoodie, "here take this" I say handing her my hoodie and saying "page me when you get home."

I get to my grandmother house wondering what I can tell her, I aint feel good..naw she's going to want me to stay in the house. It was a fire.. naw she would of heard about it on the news. End up I didnt have to tell her nothing because she wasn't in there, she went to a clinic appointment and my father was holding down the house.

"What you doin here so early son?" My father asked.

"Man they had a fire drill and had the whole school standin outside in the cold, I ain't have no jacket or nothing, so I got outta there I wasn't gettin sick fuckin wit no fire drill," I tell my father.

"Well granny at the clinic, she should be back in a lil while."

"Ard well imma jus grab a jacket an i'll be back around three, three thirty. What granny don't know won't hurt her," I say then ran up stairs to grab a jacket and the couple 100 pills i bagged up lastnite. Fuck it, I might as well grab some ounces for them niggas to bag up.

(BACK IN THE CAR WITH O)

"Yo, you heard yo got merked lastnite?" I asked O.

"Heard, yeah I heard" he says with a slight smirk.

"I bagged up two ounces, I got about 350 pills plus I grabbed another two ounces for dem niggas to bag up."

"Thats cool, imma cook another joint up when I go in the house. Imma bring it back out here tonite, you goin to sell them ones you bagged up or you giving it to them niggas?"

"I probably sell half of em I need some money for real."

"Yeah I gotta give you that five hunnit I owe you, look take 200 of them pills and jus give me a stack off it, jus give the other 150 to T-Rod. Him, Manna and Bean in Vick house, jus give the other 2 ounces to Manna and Bean.

"You ain't goin in?" I asked.

"Naw, I gotta take care of something I will be back tonite tho, keep a gun close by yall jus in case yall need it."

'Aight, I see you when you get back," I say then I get out of the car.

I go in Vick's house and give them niggas the work, I chill for a minute then me and T-Rod hit the block.

"Yo you strapped?" I asked.

"If it ain't on ya hip then you lookin ta die," he says repeating a line off the new L.O.X album.

"Yo what we goin do put the pills up Robo's and bring them down 50 at a time?" I ask.

"Yeah we can do it like that," he says.

As soon as we came out of Robo's, money started coming from everwhere. "Give me 10", "give me 8", "can I get 17 for 150?" Niggas ain't even have time to stash the first 50 pills, by the time we finished serving the crowd we only had 3 left out that first 50.

Me and T-Rod started the 350 pills at a little before 12PM by 3PM we were working on the last 50 pills and its good we were finishing up because Manna and Bean were coming thru the parking lot about to stash their pills.

"How many baby?" I ask an approaching fiend.

"Give me four nephew, where the books at?" She asked while we were making the exchange.

"Today was jus one of those days", I tell her briefly replaying the last few days in my head.

I felt she saw the sincerity in my answer as she replied back, "aight, imma give you that one nephew jus don't let one of those days turn into one of those weeks and those weeks turn into one of those years cuz before you know it ten years been done passed you by," she says as she walks off.

"Yo one time comin thru the parking lot" Manna yells joggin towards us.

"Hurry up run up Robo's Scotty," Tyrod tells me since I had the gun and about 30 pills on me it seemed like a good idea.

I peek out of Robo's window as soon as I get up there I see the police harrassing T-Rod and Manna, Bean must of ran. He known for gettin low on the police even if he ain't dirty he still runs. Anyway this is whats going on with Manna and T-Rod.."put your god danm hands on the wall!," the cop says to Manna and t-Rod as his four dickhead partners circle the perimises.

"Yall got any guns or drugs on yall? Jus tell me now cuz if I search you and find it im goin have ta fuck you boys up, now with that said am I goin find anything?"

"Man don't nobody got shit on em, what yall fuckin wit us for," Tyrod says.

"Yall The Wallboys, thats reason enough right there. Search em real good now boys," the Sarge instructs the rest of his dickheads.

The two searching Manna and T-Rod remind me of Ernie and bert off Sesame Street, the letter for the day is..A for assholes.

"Sarge they ain't got no guns or drugs on em but they got plenty money on em tho," Bert says to his Sergent.

"Let me have a look," "see" "well goddanm! This more than a months salary, what you boys doin with all this money?"

"I work, I jus got my income taxes," Tyrod tells the Sarge.

"Oh we got the wrong guys, these working men here boys, where you guys work at crack Donald's sellin big cracks?"

"Over a million served huh Sarge?" Ernie slides in.

"Umm hm, The Wallboys..what yall know bout that killin happened last night?"

"We don't know nuffin and we ain't doin nuffin," Manna tells the Sarge.

Sarge responds back cockily but non-chalantly, "now we can do this one or two ways, the easy way or the hard way, its yall choice."

"I don't care which way you do it, we don't know nuffin and we ain't doin nuffin," Tyrod states as he puts his belongings back in his pocket.

"Fuck it, cuff em," Sarge instructs Ernie and Bert.

Tyrod and Manna instantly turn and push the officers standin behind them then turn and take off running. The one Tyrod pushed fell and the one Manna pushed almost went down but was caught by Sarge, boy were they mad. The two officers that weren't checking Tyrod and Manna took off after T-Rod, Bert took off after Manna. Ernie must of twisted his ankle because he got up limping. The Sarge balanced Ernie with one hand and called back up with the other.

Manna darted across the grass and thru the parking lot stutter stepping on his way out to be sure he would't get hit by a car or bus as he darts across the street to the open field with Burt in pursuit about a city block behind Manna as manna runs into the row houses where there's many twistes and turns. He see's Jennifer on her porch, he looks back and sees Bert no where in sight.

"Open the door for me Jennifer," Manna says out of breath.

They both go in Jennifer's house and lock the door.

"Im in pursuit, suspect heading southbound on Carver Rd, one of the officers breathes into his walkie talkie as he and his partner flea behind Tyrod. Tyrod leading by about a half of block still running southbound when two blue and white cars come scurrrddddding thru the intersection, each car stopping to let it's passenger out. Tyrod running almost directly to them gives his best Emmit Smith juke move faking left and cutting back right. It puts a little space between him and his two new pursuers, now heading towards the school Tyrod tries to jump the 10 ft fence but is snatched to the ground by his collar then stomped by his purs-eres. Out of breathe all Tyrod can do is block his head as their boots go to work on his ribs, waist, legs, ankles and whatever else they can stomp on. About a minute or two later Sarge and Ernie pull up right after the police finished stompin T-Rod and cuffing him.

They had to take T-Rod to the hopital before they took him to book-ing due to the beating they put on him.

"Let me have a word with him alone doc," Sarge says walking into the room at the hospital were Tyrod is cuffed to the bed.

"What you come to finish what ya goons started," Tyrod says to Sarge as he walks in.

"You started this not me!" The sarge barks, "my deputy danm near broke his ankle thanks to that stunt you and speedy gonzilas pulled."

"Well you wasting ya time if its an apology you want cuz thats out the fuckin question, my ribs danm near broke, fuck ya deputies ankle."

"Slow down, slow down, lets not get off on the wrong foot. I came to make a deal, I heard you kept your mouth shut about my boys stomping you now I was gonna charge you with assault on a officer and a bunch of other trumped up charges but fuck it im respecting your code of silence and dropping the charges. I guess we'll jus call it even," Sarge says to Tyrod as he unhooks the handcuffs from the bed, but we still owe your homeboy a ass whipping for running so let him know he got a ass whip-ping coming when we catch him." Sarge says then leaves the room.

CHAPTER 11'S INTRO

After sitting in Robo's for a half hour I paged Manna, Poka and Lil Greezy and told Robo to tell them niggas I said come up the wall. I left the gun in Robo's and took the thirty pills with me. When Manna came up there he told me Jennifer had let him hide in her house when the police chased him, supposedly one thing led to another and he ended up fucking her (supposedly. Poka and Lil Greezy said they were down the bitches house T-Rod had put them on on Valentine's Day. Manna sold one of the bagged up ounce's and Poka and Lil Greezy sold the other one together and split the profit. Robo yelled out of his window and told us T-Rod was on the phone. T-Rod filled us in on what had happend with him he said P-olie was on stand-by to come and get him when he called. He said they should be releasing him in a couple hours. Later that night O came and got the last 5 ounces I had in my house and he gave me another 40 and a half ounces. He told me to give 4 and a half to a nigga that hustled down the hill the other 36 ounces were for us. A few days went by, Row wasn't coming out as much, T-Rod was all wrapped and bandaged up so he was more so chilling on some laying low in the house shit. Sarge caught up with Manna but they didn't fuck him up tho, probably because it was an audience around when they caught up to him. Manna said he had about 700 dolllars on him and Sarge hatin ass said he would help him double his money then ripped each bill in half the whole 7 hunnit. I ain't seen O's brother Reem since the night we were all in Robo's but me, Manna, Poka, Bean, Lil Grezzy and P-olie held shit down because the block started super jamming.

Collectively we were making about $7,500 a day give or take a thousand or two depending on how the police were acting. Shit I only been hustling for a little over a week and I had 3200 saved up for myself. I know it isn't much but with no kids and no bills I was cool. The whole click was straight everybody had a few thousand saved. Since T-Rod was too hurt to hustle we all paid him to bag up ounces for us. T-Rod eventually got tired of being in the house all week so we walked up Keyco's so he could get some fresh air.

CHAPTER 11
THE INVITE

"Wut's up Keyco, I heard over the intercom that you dropped 26 points last game for the school" I say as Keyco opens his front door for me and T-Rod.

"Yeah, I don't know why you ain't sign up for the team, me and you runnin the 1 and 2 guard would be unstoppable" he replied.

"Tell me about it but all my spare time I be..you know," I say with a little embarresment for some reason.

"What's up T-Rod, how those ribs feel? I heard the police Rodney kinged ya ass, I been tryna get down there to holla at you but with school, practice and shit I ain't been able to make it." Keyco says.

"Don't trip I been mostly laid up wit my bitch, I got her feedin me grapes and shit." T-Rod says.

"So you pimpin like me then huh?" Keyco replies.

"Aw man, you light skin niggas kill me all yall pimpin, yall two Lil Grezzy and Big Greezy. I guess im the only sucka for love huh?" I say grabbing the playstation contoller and un-pausing the game.

"Yall darkskin niggaz jus mad cause we takin all the bitches," T-Rod says while slappin hands wit Keyco.

"I ain't mad at nobody, I...aww c'mon! Catch da danm ball, you wide open," I say to the game.

"Don't fuck up my stats you playin on my season yo," Keyco tells me.

"You playin a season and ain't runnin wit the Ravens, what kind shit you on?" I asked.

"I love the home team but im diehard Cowboys" Keyco says.

"Well start this over so I can kick your Cowboys ass wit these Ravens."
Keyco beat the shit outta me 58 to 24!

"Man you cheated, you think I don't know you put the code in? Ain't
No way Emmit old ass runnin like that on the Ravens, im goin outside to
smoke me a cigarette," I say opening the door.

While im on the porch I see Glenn's baby mother Chadae and her two
homegirls Nelly and Rebe.

"What's up Chadae? I ain't seen yall since the funeral," I say.

"Who fault is that, my address ain't changed! Since Glenn got locked
up yall act like yall don't fuck wit us. But im glad I ran into you cuz Glenn
called me this morning and told me to tell yall he got a bail and he want
to know can yall pay it?"

"Yeah..hell yeah, how much is his bail?"

"He said it's $50,000 but you only have to pay 10%, he gave me a bail
bondsman that will take 5% but I left the number in the house."

"Aight, imma get everybody to give me some money to it, tell em we
goin get em out."

"Damn Scotty, what Chardae the only one you speakin to taday?"

"Yeah, I mean what the fuck we invisible or sumthin?"

"I tell you how quick people change," Nelly and Marie went back and
forth grilling me.

"Yo don't even do dat, I was jus ready holla at yall soon as Chardae finish."

"Don't put that on me nigga," Chardae cuts me off taking sides with
her homegirls.

"Danm you goin switch up that quick?" I ask Chardae.

"Ya damn skippy," she replied.

"Yo who's that?" T-Rod and Keyco ask comin out the house." Oh was-
sup yall, what's up Chardae was up Nelly, was up Rebe," T-Rod and Keyco
say from the porch.

"What's up T-Rod and Keyco," they all speak back.

"Yall need to teach Scotty some manners," Rebe says

"Umm hmm" Nelly joins in.

"That's crazy now yall got me feelin bad, where yall goin be tonight?
Drinks on me," I said trying to end the exchange on a good note (didn't work).

"Don't lie to us," Chardae says.

"Yeah don't lie to us, or we'll cut cha dick off." Rebe says.

"Wut the fuc.." I mumble to myself caught off guard, "anyway where yall goin be, around Chardae's?" I asked.

"Yeah we'll be there, will you?" Nelly asked as they strut off.

"What the fuck was that about?" Tyrod asked.

"Fuck if I know, they geekin oh Chardae said Glenn got a bail he need five thou or something like that," I said to T-Rod while sparking a cigerette.

"Yo you jus smoked a cigerette," Keyco says to me.

"I know, I need some weed or imma keep smokin cigerettes."

"I got a stack to Glenn bail, everybody goin have to put something up but we can pull him tonight!" T-Rod says.

"Scotty, t-Rod, what do we owe de pleasure," Jah Keyco's Jamacian step faher says as he walks into the yard.

"We come ta see if you had some of that good green yall be smokin in da Island," T-Rod says ending his sentence with a bad Jamaican accent.

"Fuck you know bout de I-lands, no offense Keyco but we run you light skin Bumboclaat off De Islands years ago," Jah says joking with T-Rod.

"I was jus tellin these niggas the same shit Jah, dat pretty boy shit played out," I say agreeing with Jah.

"You know how long it take Keyco to get ready in da morning? 2 fuckin hours!" Jah says

"Unfuckin believable!" I say in a loud outburst.

"Why you guys out here in da cold, me body not use to dis shit its warm in De Islands."

"Scotty smokin dem cancer sticks," Keyco says as he opens the door.

I throw my cigerette and we all go in house, Jah goes upstairs and we stay in the living room.

"Let me play Tyrod yo, you a fuckin hulk Keyco. You know can't no-body beat you in this shit," I say referring to the game.

"You called me out?" Keyco asks.

"Where that shootin game at? You know I can't play this football shit," Tyrod says.

We go to war in some head to head shooting game for about 45 minutes then Jah comes back downstairs and throws about a half ounce of some of the prettiest weed you ever seen on the coffee table and said,

"yall have dat best I can do I don't have no endless supply of weed, I got endless supply of dope. Ty if you and Scotty take my dope up your wall, sky is de limit." Jah says.

"We don't know nuffin bout no dope," Tyrod says.

"I'll teach you every blood clot ting you need to know," Jah says.

"Sniff Sniff, man this shit look like if you cut the lights out this shit a glow in da dark!" I say tryna change the subject.

"Yeah, propa ting I can't smoke dat shit dey sellin out here."

Beep! Beep! Beep...Beep! Beep! Beep!

"Aw shit this Manna, where the phone at Keyco" I say while checking my pager.

Keyco gets the cordless phone from upstairs.

"What's up, what u ain't comin out?" Manna ask thru the phone.

"Yeah im comin up there, who up there? I gotta holla at yall about somethin anyway."

"Me, Bean and Poka up Robo's, P-olie and Lil Grezzy went ta get food and blunts."

"Aight, I be up there in a minute let me finish hollerin at T-Rod and Keyco."

"Aight, tell them niggas I said what up!" Manna says before he hangs the phone up.

"Yo Manna holler'd at yall niggas," I tell T-Rod and Keyco then ask T-Rod," you chillin down here for a while?"

"Yeah imma put a blunt of that glow in the dark in me then finish bustin Keyco ass in this game."

"Aight well we jus goin split the grass now cuz im bouta go up The Hill and see what niggas got to this bail."

I dumped T-Rods half of the weed onto a Playstation game case and put the sandwich bag in my pocket.

"Aight thanks for da grass Jah, I see you niggas when I see you niggas," I say as I slap hands and leave.

"Don't forget, sky's de limit!" I hear Jah say as im shutting the door.

When I get up The Wall I see Robo standing outside hitting sales.

"What up solider Robo greets me as I approach, them niggaz upstaris he tells me.

"You good out this bitch by yourself?" I ask him.

Yeah im good solider, them niggaz went upsrtairs to warm up for a minute. I'm good Robo says and pulls a pint of Black Watch Vodka out his jacket,

"aight be careful!" I say then walk towards his building.

"Scotty! Ayy Scotty!" I heard some one calling in the distance, I look back and see Jennifer and Jessica walking towards me.

"You seen Manna?" Jennifer asked.

"So yall just using me to get to Manna?" I say joking.

"You know we fucks wit you Scotty," Jessica says. Yeah I know, i'm just fucking wit yall, Manna upstairs c'mon."

When we get upstairs these niggaz got guns and drugs all on the living room table.

"Oh my god, im not goin in there."

"What?" Manna asked looking confused.

"Why yall just got guns layin around like that?" Jennifer asks.

"Better safe than sorry." Bean tells her.

"Yo, look what I came across," I say whipping the weed out I got from Jah.

"Let me see," Bean says.

"What yall goin do, yall comin in or what? Manna asked Jennifer and Jessica.

"Well we just wanted to tell yall we're having a party at The Patapsco Arena on Friday and we wanted yall to come!" Jennifer says handing Manna a flyer.

"Is that it," Manna asks.

"Yeah that's it, for now anyway!" Jennifer says.

"Page me later," Manna tells Jennifer as she turns to leave.

"Yo, where you get this grass from Scotty? THIS THAT!!!" Bean says breaking up one of the buds.

"Let me see it!" Manna says locking the door then says, "damn this shit do look good. Oh Scotty your mother came up here, she tried to buy something at first I wasnt going to serve her but then I aint want her to go no where else and have to buy nothing and one one of them other niggaz disrespect her or something not knowing who she is long story short I ended up just giving them to her. I know you don't like her getting high but she a grown woman like it or not she is goin to do what she wanna do. So I just did the samething I would of did if it was my mother."

"That's some real shit and I be telling her not to come up here, but you right cuz if one of them niggaz jump out there on my mother shorty imma go off."

"I already know" Manna says." "Yo, but what you had to holla at everybody about."

"Oh yeah, I seen Chardae when I was down Keyco house, she said Glenn got a bail and he need $5,000 all together, T-Rod said he got a stack, I got a stack so we need 3 more thousand." I tell them.

"Aight, we goin get the rest of the money together when everybody get up here."

"Woo!!! Don't nobody go in the bathroom for about 35-45 minutes and somebody open a window in this bitch." Poka says coming out the bathroom. I thought I heard you out here Scotty, I heard some bitch's too, where the bitchs at?" Poka asks.

"They left, they having a party over Patapsco Friday. We gotta go up Mondawmin to get fresh we can get O or P to take us cuz i'm ready to sell my car, that bitch over heating, unda heating and somemore shit!" Manna says.

"Why don't you get my grandfather to fix it?" I ask Manna.

"Cuz I dont want us to become unbenefit when I shoot your grandfather for fucking up my Cadi."

"How he goin fuck up something that's already fucked up?"

"Naw, I already know what's wrong wit it im just not gettin it fixed, im sellin it, fuck it."

"Fuck it."

CHAPTER 12'S INTRO

P-olie dropped me off in the house that weed had me numb and I was stupid high. I never made it to chill with Chardae and them. We all put up for Glenn's bail and P said he would drop the money off to Glenn's mother. It was a Tuesday night when P-olie gave the money to Glenn's mother, she bailed him out Wednesday morning so he didn't get out until about 10 something that night. O went and picked him up and dropped him off so he could get his nuts out the sand. I skipped school the next morning which I've been doing a lot lately I noticed. I left out 7:30 in the morning like I normally do but instead of going to the bus stop or my hack's house I went up Robo's. I still had about two blunts worth of that glow in the dark weed, so I sent Robo to the store for me to get a box of Dutch's, a sausage, egg, and cheese sandwich with a Everfresh orange juice. I told him to get what he wanted which I knew would be a pint of Black Watch. When he got back from the store I smoked, ate, and then gave Robo 25 pills and he hit the block for me. After eating and smoking a half of blunt of that glow in the dark I fell asleep on his couch.

CHAPTER 12

Party & Bullshit

"Look at this nigga, you in here with your feet up, shoes off, sleep!" Glenn says as him, Manna, and Robo come thru Robo's apartment door. "Every shut eye ain't sleep nigga." I say as I take my hand from under the couch's pillow to reveal my 380 I've been clutching the whole time I was sleep. I leave the gun on the couch and stand up and slap hands and man hug my nigga." I ain't been gone a year and look at you nigga, you was barely hustlin before I left. Now you tot'n guns, holdin the block down." Glenn says to me enthusiasticlly. "Yeah man, I feel like my niggaz needed me up here. Wit Fezie dying..Yall niggaz gettin locked up, but look at you though still the same pretty boy you were before you left. Design braids and shit, first thing this nigga do when he comes home is getting his fuckin hair done, Unbelievable!" I say.

"Man, I had these braids in for about a week."

"A week?" I say confused then inquiring more.

"Hold up, hold up, who did them braids?"

"A lil nigga on the tier."

"A lil nigga on the tier! What the fuck you let a nigga do ya hair?" I say outraged, also a little confused because I know Glenn is a stand up dude.

"How the fuck I'm suppose to get it done?" He questions."

"I don't know, I just....I don't know.... man Fuck that shit." I say. "What is it nigga?"

"Aw man, I can't call it, i'm just happy to be back."

"Well we most definitely happy to have you back." "

Scotty where that shit at? I know you got some more of that grass from last night." Manna says.

"Yeah, I got a blunt of that shit left. Yo I know you goin to the party tomorrow?" I ask Glenn.

"Yeah, Manna was just telling me about that shit on the way up here. Yall tryin to hit the mall now? I can call my hack man and see if he will take us." I say.

"Let's wait until school ready to let out, you know its goin be bitch's in there then! Plus O might come out here by then."

"Man, if you don't gas up that Cadi, keep actin like you can't drive that mufucka."

We bullshitted around Robo's until about 3 o'clock nobody came up there but Poka so far. Manna said fuck it he would drive to the mall. So me, Manna, Glenn, and Poka rode up Mondawmin Mall smoking and tripping.

"Damn we got up here just in time it's bitches everywhere!" Glenn says.

"Honk, Honk," Manna honks the horn at four girls walking past the car as we are trying to park.

"Don't think cuz yall cute I won't run yall over." Manna says as we all get out the car. "

Damn, first I get dumped on my birthday now you want to run me over, what a day!" One of the girls say as we approach them.

"I know ain't noboby dump your sexy ass, yo must of been a lame to do some shit like that." Manna tells her then asks, "what's your name anyway?"

"Crystal!" The girl reply's.

"Well I'm Manna, and this Glenn, that's Scotty, and that's Poka. Won't you introduce them to your friends."

"That's Keona, that's Tasha, and that's Nee-Nee." (We all speak and they speak back)

"So what we goin to stand out here and freeze to death?" I ask sarcastically.

"Naw, come on yall, let's make it a Happy Birthday for the irthday girl," Manna says and starts walking towards the mall. When we get in the mall we go into some store that sells nothing but girls/womens clothes.

First, I'm tripping in my head off this nigga Manna. When the fuck did he become Mr. Nice Guy? Then I tell myself fuck it, you can't beat em join em.

"Ay Tarsha, your about my sisters size, what size do you wear?

Help me pick some shit out for her, I got you," I say. I was high and I didn't remember at first that Glenn only had a couple of dollars on him so he couldn't really stunt out. I mean we were going to pay for what ever he was going to buy but now we stuntin he gotta stunt too. So me, Poka, and Manna gave Glenn $250 a piece. Girl clothes don't cost much at least not in this store anyway. Shit, I got tarsha 3 outfits and she picked out 3 outfits for my girl.

Wait I mean "my sister". (Let me let yall in on a little secret Readers. Don't tell tarsha, but I don't really have a sister. Those outfits she picked out were for Angie but back to what I was saying!) The 6 outfits only came up to about $140 which wasn't bad. So from the girls store we went to the USA Boutique to get our clothes for the party. I bought a smoked gray Iceberg sweatsuit with Marvin The Martian on the hoody, and I paid $240 for that. It was a zip up hoody so I had to get the Iceberg t-shirt to go under the hoody, $40 fo that. Poka bought some blue Azzure jeans wit golden/yellow stichen goin thru the jeans for $90.

He brought a yellow Polo shirt, it was a long sleeve that button all the way down for $115. Manna has us about to put our shit back and buy something different when he bought the all black Coogi knit sweater that mufucka was $275 by itself and that was the sale price. He bought some jeans, he ain't really care too much about the jeans as long as they were boot cut but he still end up paying about 8$0 for what ever the brand of the jeans were. Glenn bought a classic grey Shooters sweatsuit with Shooters spelled in rainbow colors across the zip up hoody. The sweatsuit only cost him $150 but he a pretty boy.

The price didn't matter he was going to be fly regardless. Then we went to the shoe store and bought kicks to accent our outfits for the party. We all put up 20 dollars to the birthday girl tennis shoes but she was the only one we bought shoes for they all got free clothes, after the shoe store we went to the Food Court and all ate together. Nothing expensive like with the Slater Girls, this was just Chicken Strips and shit like that.

I had the munchies so I had to get me some Snicker Doodles from The Great Cookie, I always get them when I come to Mondawmin. Glenn bought a beeper and we gave the girls our pager numbers before we parted ways.

(On the ride back to the hood we was still trippin.)

"Remind me never to go shoppin wit yo again." I say nodding my head in Manna's direction.

"Yeah, yo jumped all the way out there didn't he, let's make it a Happy Birthday for the birthday girl!" Poka joins in joking Manna wit me.

"He the same nigga quick to call me a sucka for love." I say.

"Yo, I didn't tell yall buy them bitch's nothing and Scotty you a bluffin mufucka talkin bout "my sister about ya size" you don't even have no fuckin sister!" Manna says.

"Well at least yall ain't buy the bitch's no tennis the clothes was cool, I only spent $60 on Keona's shit." Glenn says.

"Yeah that's all I spent forreal plus the other $20 Manna got from me for Crystal's tennis Poka says, that bitch Nee-Nee better page me."

"Them bitch's goin to hit us, I bet $50 one of them bitch's page one of us before the night out." Manna says.

(I spark a cigarette and kick back the rest of the ride.)

(When we get back in Robo's O's up there P-olie's in there sippin on a pint of Hennessy with Bean and Lil Greezy. We walk in the door still trippin off the bitch's we met.)

"I wouldn't of never jumped out there if them bitch's was ugly, but keep it real all them bitch's looked good." Manna says as we walk in the living room. "Damn, niggaz go shopping and don't tell nobody," Bean says.

"We had been up here all morning waiting for yall niggaz to come out. It ain't our fault niggaz don't come outside til 4 o'clock." Manna says.

"P or O could take yall niggaz up there and get some shit anyway I don't know how many niggaz suppose to fit in one car but we was already four deep in the Cadi." Manna complained.

"What yall bought yall shit for the party?" O asked grabbing our bags looking in them.

"Yeah, you goin O?" I ask.

"Yeah, my niggaz there I'm there, me and P can take the rest of yall to the mall. Page Row and T-Rod and see if they goin."

"I bet Row bring his dumb ass wit us this time." Lil Greezy says.

———

Friday night we're in the parking lot about to go in the spot where the party is but we're finishing off the last of our liqure and checking our fresh.

"Yo, I should zip my hoodie up? Or I should rock it open?" I say to anyone listening. "Leave it open shorty." O says to me. "So what we going to leave all the guns in the cars?" Manna asked

"They checkin niggaz at the door P asked?" "We should of got Jennifer and them to bring our shit in earlier while they were setting the food up & shit." O says.

"You think they goin check the hood of my hoodie? I probably could put the 380 or the 25 in there,"glenn says.

"I don't know, you might could get away with it. Yall think we need the joints in the club?' "They probably aight in the whips." P says. "Fuck it, leave em in the cars," O says finalizing the matter.

Me, glenn, and manna rode together. We left the 380 and the 38 in the cadi.

"O", Row, and Poker rode together they had a 25 in the TL with them and row had a P-89. They left both joints in the car. P-olie, Bean, and lil greezy rode together. Lill greezy didn't bring his sawed off all they had in the whip with them was s snub nose 357. the two 9mm's seem to have just disappeared.

Anyway the party was from 9pm until 2am. We got in there at about 11:15 it was alot of people there but not so crowded that you couldn't move around. We went in and found two tables.

C'mon glenn, let's hit the bar. I say over the music. We all been drinking Jack Daniels all night in memory of fezie that was his shit and this is the first party we been to without him.

At the bar we run into glenn's baby mother and her home girls and Marie starts dancing with me until Nelly grabs her off of me.

"Uh-un re, we don't dance with liars." I hear Nelly say over the music. "Yeah, you owe us drinks," Marie says while taking my cup out of my hand.

"Yall already fuck'd up. No don't drink tha......." I tried to stop Marie before she downed my cup but I was to late. I ain't give a fuck about the drink. I just ain't think she could handle a whole cup of Jack and coke. Wrong, she killed my shit. I see glenn dancing with his "BM" so I walk Marie and Nelly to the bar.

"Yo, we drinking Jack all night for fezie." I say. "Oh, that's what the shit was that shit's strong, but bring it on baby," Marie says and say as I see P walking to the bar. "You know Nelly and Marie?" I ask P. "Yeah, I seen em at Ki-Ki's after the funeral,'" he says.

"4 Jack and coke's." the barmaid says. We all grab a cup. "To Fezie," P says holding his cup out. "To Fezie!" we all say and hit cups and take gulps of our drink. "Now, to the dance floor,"Marie says grabbing my arm leading me thru the crowd. Me and Marie danced thru about two songs then I looked up to see manna calling me back to our table.

"What's up," I say as I get back to our table. "Yo, we're about to take some pictures,"manna tells me. "Everybody ain't even over here," I say.

"Where the fuck does lil greezy think he at?" O says. I look in the crowd and lil greezy's in his tank top with his collar shirt in his had swinging it over his head like a helicopter with about three girls around him, lil glenn throws a arm around his neck and shoulder and escorts him back to our tables. I saw P-olie and poka over by the bar, "let me run and get them," I say. "I'm goin wit you Scotty," bean says.

We go get poka and P and two cups of Jack while we over there. Then we all go to the picture booth and pose for about 3 pictures then out of no where the slater girls jump in front of the camera with us for about 7 more pictures then we all took a solo shot. After we finished taking pictures we were still chilling by the picture booth laugh'n and joking with the slater girls when Chardae and Marie came over there and put their arms around me and glenn and said. "Yall coming wit us tonight ?" The look the slater girls gave them two gave me a chill, but Chardae and Marie didn't seem to notice or care because they just ushered us off. Once we got a few feet away from the crowd they popped the question again.

"I mean what the fuck! was we talking to ourselves or yall was just scared to answer around yall groupies," Chardae says." Are yall coming wit us?" Glenn looks at me. I strugg my shoulders letting him know it's whatever wit me. Then he strugg his shoulders to let me know the same thing. "How you getting home?" Glenn asked Chardae. "Marie's sister drove us over here and she taking us back."

"Well me and Scotty goin to get dropped off over your house after the party. Marie stayin wit you?" Glenn asked. "Yeah, she stayin over there and yall better come cuz I really don't feel like fuckin yall slater girls up." "Man shut up." Glenn tells Chardae.

"Boy don't get cute. Buy us some drinks or yall gotta get back to yall groupies?" "Excuse me yall, let me borrow Scotty for a minute." O says putting his arm around my neck. "What's happenin?" I ask O.

"You see the nigga right there by the speaker?" O asked in my ear so i could hear him over the music.

"Yeah that's the nigga from down the hill you told me to give the 4 and a half ounces to." i say with a confident uncertainty. "RIght, but you see the nigga he talking to wit the Jersey on?" "Yeah if I ain't mistaken yo go to my school. What's up wit the nigga tho?"i asked." Between him and his man. I fronted them niggaz almost 7 ounces." "When they give me the money for that I might need you to take them some more work". "That's it. I thought you wanted me to smoke the niggaz or something. You getting me all excited for nothing", i say eagerly probably because the liquor was starting to take effect. "Naw, I just wanted you to see who you dealing wit that's all."

"Aight, man come drink a shot of Jack wit me. I ain't seen you wit a drink all night and where's row at I ain't seem him away from the table all night. He been acting a lil different since.....you know." I say to O as we walk back to our table.

"Yeah, don't sweat that shit shorty, let's go get that shot." When we get to the bar manna and Bean are there with the slater girls. "Man, what the fuck is they drinking? Long Islands and shit. I thought everybody was drinking Jack. I even got "O" about to take a shot wit me." Me and O order two Jacks wit coke. Manna and Bean already had cups in their hand while they were talking to Jennifer and Kelly when mystikals song came thru the speaker. "Shake ya ass! Watch ya self, Shake ya ass, Show me what cha workin wit!" "Oh, this my shit!" Jessica says and drinks all that's left in her cup before she pulls me towards the dance floor. At a quarter until two the lights came on and the music played at a quieter volume while the DJ thanked everybody for coming and told everyone to drive safe.

Outside in the parking lot some girl was vanderlizing what I guess what was her boyfriend's car. The poor girl threw a brick at the window missing 3 times hitting anything but the window. The door the roof.

Then I hear in another crowd "Cause yall bitch's been askin for it all night". I hear Jennifer say to Chardae. "Bitch's!" Chardae repeats and grabs a beer bottle off the ground about to throw it when the clubs bouncer grabs her from behind and twist her wrist and she drops the bottle. As soon as the bottle hits the ground I don't know where Glenn came from but his fist catch's the bouncer across the chin. The bouncer didn't drop he just stumbled about two steps. That's when Chardae picked the top half of the broken bottle up like it was a knife she looked at the bouncer like she was about to attack him. Then she looked him off and looked back to Jennifer and her girls. "Oh, I got ya bitch right here!" Chardae says as she throws the half broken bottle just missing Jennifer's head. A second bouncer tries to rush glenn but O catch's him with a right hand to his chubby cheek. That's when we all run over there. The bitch's trying to get at each other. We're getting with the bouncer for about 5 to 10 seconds when.

Wurp! Wurp! Police come from everywhere pulling into the parking lot about 6 cars at first blocking off the only driving exit. Jumping out of there cars with there guns drawn.

Everyone retreats from the commotion, we get the fuck away from the bouncer's. The bitch's get away from each other. So we are sitting on the hoods of our cars smoking cigarette's parking lot pimping you know shit like that. The bouncer's didn't even press the issue about us give'n them a 10 second workover. So it wasn't really much the police could say about shit, but they came over to where we were at. About four of them draw guns and say,"Otis "O" Glover and Roland "Row" Henson put your hands behind you back, your under arrest". "Under arrest! under arrest for what?" O says defensively. "For the murder of Sam "Oneeye" Tyson."The cop responds with a confident smile.

———

"I swear to GOD! Them bitch's bad luck, everytime we get around them something fucked up happens," I tell Poka as me and him drive back to the hood in O's TL. He gave me the keys before they put him in the Police car. "Ain't no such thing as luck, what's goin happen is goin happen," Poka tells me. Back at Robo's were all up there drunk, mad, and confused as a mutha-fucka. "He goin to get a phone call tonight, he might call up here then it's goin to take him about 24 hours to see the commissioner to see if he gets a bail or not. Then he'll call again but we shoud know something by tomor-row or the next day," Glenn schools us. He just turned 18 the day Fezie died but he's been telling the system he 18 since he was 16 so he's familiar with the adult system. "So what the fuck niggaz doin tonight?" Manna asked.

"Me and Scotty crashing around Chardae's," Glenn says.

"Im goin over Jennifer's once everybody figure out what they doin," Manna says.

"Kelly told me throw a rock at her window, she said if her bedroom light is on she up there," Bean says.

"My girl at my house waiting so I'm goin in once I leave yall," P says.

"I ain't get to set no pussy shot up, I was goin to do that in the parking lot but wit all that was goin on I ain't set up shit so fuck it somebody just take me to get some weed. I'll stay here to see if O calls." Poka says.

"Fuck it, it look like I'm here too it's 2:30 I definitely can't go over my bitch house. Looks like imma have to hit you tonight Poka," Lil Greezy says joking. "C'mon yo somebody ride down the weed strip wit me it's the weekend them niggaz still out. They just in the buildings probably." Poka says as he grabs a gun of the table and heads towards the door.

(We went and got some weed and then everybody went on their seperate mission.)

"Ahhh! Oh my GOD, how'd yall get in here?" Chardae says as we walk thru her bedroom door.

"Yall drunk asses ain't even lock the door," Glenn tells her and Marie.

"What they lock O and Row up for?"

Marie asked.

"We don't really know yet," Glen says lying then I change the subject by asking, "Ain't no trash can up here Chardae? Where am I supposed to dump all these blunt guts at?" I say crackin a dutch.

"Dump em in the toilet!" Chardae says.

I rolled the weed up, lit it, hit it a couple of times, and then passed it to Glenn. He hit the blunt twice then dropped it in the ashtray and ran straight to the bathroom after Chardae hit the blunt she went to check on Glenn. They closed the bathroom door and after about 5 minutes of the water running you heard, "Ooh ooh........Ahhh ahhh!" And all other kinds of moans and smacks and gushes.

Around this time I grab the blunt from Marie with one hand then she grabs my other hand and stuck it down her pants so I could see how wet she was, this instantly got me hard and I had on sweatpants!

She saw my reaction bulging thru the fabric in my pants so then she reached her hand in my pants and starting stroking my "Ego". I dropped the blunt in the ashtray and was about to pull her pants all the way Off, they were already unbuttoned so I grabbed the hip of her pants and she put her hand on my hand and said, "lock the door!" They say Jack Daniels is a Cowboys drink and I must agree cuz I fucked the cowboy shit out of her. Machine gun fuckin her doggy style on the edge of the bed, she is moanin ("uhhhhh..ahhhhh") and I'm givin it to her real rough, and I'm talkin shit. ("Um hmm, take that!")

Um, um, um, um, um, smack! her ass, then I wipe the sweat out my eye with her shirt and then I wipe her face without stopping my stroke. I looked and seen the half of blunt still in the ashtray with a lighter right next to it. Then I hit the superman pose wit my hands at my hips wit my fist closed still hittin all waist action. Then I say, "look Re no hands."

"You go boy, I see you," she says as she looks back then re-adjust her hands then start throwin her ass on like a sideways angle making me have to find another rhythm. No problem, I throw one leg up on the bed,

then reached across her lower back and grab the blunt and the lighter, I didn't even light the blunt immediately cuz her body looked so sexy laid across the bed with her carmel colored ass in the air. She started to back it up slow as I finally hit the blunt.

CHAPTER 13'S INTRO

O's brother came out Sunday to holler at us. He said O and Row were denied bail. He said most lawyer offices weren't open on the weekend so he would start talking to some lawyers on Monday. He said everything was still going to run the same way. All the prices would stay the same. We would be seeing more of him since O was locked up. I told Reem to ask O about the 2 niggaz he pointed out in the club cuz I think they owe some money. I gave reem O's car back, but having the TL all day Saturday made me want one for myself. Other then O and Row being locked up everything was everything so we thought anyway.

The week went by pretty smooth. The bitch's we had me up the mall had paged us. We all gave them bitch's Cobo's number. So we would talk to them here and there. The block was still jamming. I had about 18 ounces in the house and the weekend was coming so I know we would knock about 10 of them out by Monday. Reem had found "O" and Row's lawyer took his case for 22,000 and Row's lawyer said he would represent him for 18,500. Both lawyers wanted a 5,000 down payment before they started. So Reem gave them that. Then we had to kick out another 18,000 to the connect for the brick he fronted. Reem said that O told him the down the hill niggaz owe up 6,200 and we were to collect that as soon as possible. I guess it ain't no time like the present cuz me and reem rode down the hill to see what was up wit that money.

CHAPTER 13
Under New Management

"That's him right there wit the Pelle Pelle leather on, I don't see the other nigga but that's one of em." I say to Reem as we pull up down the hill.

"Ay, let me holla at you for a minute champ." Reem says to the nigga as he steps out of the car. I cock the 380 and put it on safety then put it in my jacket pocket as I get out the car. "Yo, O sent me down here to holla at you, he said you was suppose to have something for him." Reem says to the nigga in the Pelle Pelle.

"Man, I've been trying to page that nigga all week," Pelle Pelle says.

"Well I'm here now so you can just give it to me champ," Reem said with a stiff smile on his face.

"Naw, that's why I wanted to holla at O cuz shit had got fucked up."

"Oh, shit got fucked up?" Reem repeats rubbing his thumb and index finger thru his chin hair.

"Yeah, I was goin to try and work something out with him, see if he wou......."

"Man fuck all that!" Reem interrupts, "what the fuck you think a nigga playin about that money?" I step around to the same side of the car that Reem was on and put my hand in my jacket pocket and took the safety off.

About three of Pelle Pelle's homeboys walked over to where we were.

"Yo, you good?" One of them asked Pelle Pelle. "Yeah, I'm good, like I was sayin im tryin to holla at O main man! Me and you ain't got no business together." Pelle pelle tells Reem. I looked at Reem without saying a word, my eyes asked him (to squeeze or not to squeeze?) that's the question.

"You right homeboy O got your number right?" Reem says as he turns and reaches for his car door.

"Yeah he got it!" Pelle pelle says real gully.

"Aight, Reem says with a smile, I walk to the passenger side of the car without fully turning my back on the small crowd with my hand on the trigger the whole time.

(We pulled off and headed back up The Hill!)

"That's all you had to do was nod ya head in his direction and I would of aired his bitch ass out," I say to Reem as I take the 380 out of my jacket pocket and put it on my lap.

"Yeah that's why we had to get the fuck away from there or we was goin be over there wit Row and O," Reem says.

(We get back up The Wall and tell the rest of the click what happened.)

"I knew I should of went down there wit yall," Manna says.

"Shorty that wouldn't of changed nothing, Scotty did exactly what he was suppose to do and I did what was in all our best interest. You really think imma let that bitch ass nigga get away with that stunt he just pulled? If anybody up here know better than that it's you Manna!" Reem says.

"I need some grass don't none of yall got no weed?" I ask.

"Poka up Robo's smoking," Bean says.

"I don't even want no weed, take me up the store Reem so I can grab a 1/2 pint or something." Bean says.

"Come on," Reem responds.

"I'm riding," Lil Greezy says.

"Get me a Hot Chocolate." I say and then I walk up Robo's.

"Where he at?" "He just walked thru the door," Poka says into the phone. "Who's that ?" I ask.

"Nee-Nee said Tarsha got some words for you."

"I hope one of them words is fuckin, let me hit that grass." I say taking my jacket off throwin it on the couch.

"What's up soldier?" Robo says coming out of his room.

"Give me 5 dollars shorty so I can get my drink these niggaz tight as shit." Robo says.

I go to the window and yell to Manna, "stop Reem before he pull off!" Manna stops the car.

"Yo, get Robo a 5th of Black Watch I got the money when you get back!" I yell to the car.

We normally have the same routine, hustle and bullshit up Robo's.

A little after 10 I told Reem to take me down Angie's house, she's been complaining about me neglecting her. I never even took her the 3 outfits I had got her before the party, they've been sitting in Robo's closet the whole time. Bean rode with me and Reem down Angie's house, I had my 380 with me cuz I might walk up The Hill tonight either way I'd be strapped in the morning when I left out. Them niggaz was strapped too, Reem said he was going to see if Pelle Pelle might be outside slippin. We circled his block on our way to Angie's but we ain't see nobody out, so I went to Angie's and told my nigga's I would see them in the morning.

"Ooh, you brought me something!" She says as she's letting me in.

"Yeah this crack head was selling it, if you don't like it I ain't going to be mad."

"Hi Scotty, Angie's mother says coming out of the kitchen makin her way upstairs then she backs up oh and thanks for the Valentine's Day Chocolate's. Greedy ate half of em but thank you, your such a sweetheart."

"Don't let him fool you Ma, he's the damn devil in disguise.

You know he's trying to cheat on me with our teacher."

"I don't believe that," Angie's mother says.

"Well why she ask me about him everytime he don't show up for class? Friday when she asked me I told her won't she get your fuckin pager number so she could stop askin me."

"Angie you didn't curse out your teacher?" Her mother ask.

"Fuck her she think she slick and he ain't no better buying her Valentine's Day gifts."

"Are you tryin to put the moves on your teacher Scotty?" Angie's mother ask's.

"Please don't pump her up Ms.V," I say to Angie's mother.

"Well what did he get her?" Miss V asked Angie.

"All I saw was a heart like ours but ain't no telling the ring and neck-lace might have been in her drawer."

"What did the necklace say Scotty #1 teacher?"

"I thought we were better than that Ms.V just like that you......."

"Ooh! Get away from that window yall two and get upstairs yall hear those gun shots." Miss Vanessa warns us. We go upstairs, Miss V goes in her room and I go in Angie's room with a smile on my face. I'm thinking I hope they killed Pelle pelle's bitch ass.

CHAPTER 14 INTRO

At Angie's house we heard police cars zooming around and saw an ambulance ride by from the upstairs window. Ms. Vanessa didn't think it was safe for me to leave so she called and talked to my granny and I ended up staying the night at Angie's. I had a few pieces of clothes down Angie's so I took a shower and went to school from her house the next morning. Before school we stopped at the McDonald's a block away from the school to have breakfast. Without smoking before breakfast my appetite is all fucked up, so I really just picked through my food and drank my orange juice. I love Mickey D's orange juice. On the way out of McDonald's Keyco was coming in so I talked with him for a few minutes then me and Angie went to school. We don't have the same first period class so we went our separate ways once we got in the building. I went to my locker and put my 380 in it, lately I've been leaving my books in my locker. Why keep dragging them back in forth home when the only time I use them is when im in school so why not leave em here. The day went by pretty fast, I went to every class except last period which was Biology, I hate that class. It seems like everybody hates last period, all hustlers anyway because last periold it's always a big dice game in the stairwell #6. This is the only stairwell that doesn't have video surveillance and niggaz be mobbed deep back here last period. I normally don't stay at school this long but fuck it since I'm in school this is where I am last period.

CHAPTER 14
Old Habits Die Hard

"Yo, ain't nobody got no grass for sale down here?" I ask as I enter the stairwell. "Yeah, Lil Stay High got some, he be right back but you might as well loose some of that money while you wait for him."

Shooter tells me while shaking the dice.

"What yall shootin?" I ask.

"Shootin 5, bettin 5, who don't like my four?" Shooter asks the circle surrounding the game.

"I like you for the 10-4 I say going against the odds since my whole life the odds been against me. The whole circle betted against Shooter except for me and he made them pay for it throwing two tens then a four.

"I like his come out, who don't like him?" I ask getting two people to bet against his come out and he threw an eleven as soon as our money hit the floor then he followed up with two sevens before getting a point of eight, "Six, eight, who don't like my six, eight?" Shooter ask. We bet all around the board with Shooter talkin shit the whole time.

"When I hit this number don't nobody bend down but me and Scotty!" He says shaking the dice.

"Shooter, you hungry shorty?" I ask him.

"Naw, I ain't hungry" he says rolling the dice, I just eight!" He says as the dice land on a five and a three.

"Let me get some of this money you niggaz givin away down this bitch," Stay High says turning the corner.

"Just the nigga I'm lookin for, im trying to get like you. You high as Fat Charles Ass I say to Stay High as we slap hands."

"Yo Keyco lookin for you, he said come around the gym before you dip, how many bags you want?" Stay high asked whipping out about 50 dime bags out of his hoody. I won about a hunnit and fifty dollars the 10 minutes I was at the dice game so I said fuck it let me spend the odd fifty. "Let me get 6 for 50!" We make the exchange, I slap hands with Shooter and Stay High then walk off. It was only 2:15 when I left the dice game so I said I would run to the Carryout and grab some blunts and something for me and Angie to eat, I figured if I called the food in from the pay phone I would probably have time to smoke half of one of my blunts to give me an appetite and still make it to the gym to holla at Keyco by 2:50. School don't let out until 3:00 and I didn't want to grab my 380 since I would be in the neigborhood smoking weed. No need to be strapped too so I left the gun in my locker.

"Is the order for Scotty ready?" I say to the foreigner at the counter. "2 minutes my friend I'm wrapping it up now Buddi," he says.

"Aight give me a box of Dutch's with the order but give me the blunts now." I say giving him a twenty dollar bill. I grab the Dutch's then go into the bathroom and roll one of the blunts up. I look at the time on my pager 2:33. I can work with that I say to myself exiting the bathroom. "Here you go Buddi," the foreigner says handing me my food and change. As I turn to leave the store one of the 3 niggaz comin in says "I thought that was ya bitch ass," and then throws a stiff right connecting with my left cheek.

"Bitch!" I say dropping my bag of food, throwing a right hand of my own connecting with nothing but air, as I'm hit in the temple by one of the other three then tossed 3 feet onto a table in the store by what felt like four hands.

"Imma kill one of y...I began to threaten."

"Shut up whore!" One of the three says as he catch's me right in the kisser as I'm about to get up off of the table. As I'm recovering from the punch in the mouth I see a hand dropping out of the sky gripping a pocket knife, I roll off of the table just in time to avoid the knife plunging into me. Only to land on a chair and then roll out of that. I quickly sprang back up chair in hand at the same time my foreign friend is coming around the counter with a baseball bat in hand. I cock the chair back to swing but all three of my attackers where making a run for the door.

"You alright buddi?" My foreign friend asks while he's straightening out his tables and chairs.

"Yeah, Im good I say," touching my bloody lip with my hand. I go in the bathroom and rinse my mouth out a couple of times and look at the little split in my lip. As I'm replaying the little scuffle in my mind it hits me. They were Pelle Pelle's bitch ass homeboys, I look at my pager 2:46 I gotta get back to the school so I don't miss my bus. I check inside my jacket pocket for my weed and blunt to find my blunt I rolled is ripped in half and I only have four bags of weed. I leave out of the bathroom and my foreign friend hands me my bag of food then I look under the table.

"You lookin for this my friend?" The foreigner says holding my bag of weed in his palm.

"Yeah, as a matter of fact I am." I respond.

"Can you get for me?" He asks.

"You smoke?" I immaturely ask him.

"No, no for a friend" he says.

"Well you keep that for your friend, I gotta go right now I will talk to you another time." I look left and right as I leave out of the store then I light my half of blunt telling myself, "fuck them niggaz!" I get back to the school at 2:56 the half of the blunt was gone by the time I got there. I smoked half and the wind smoked the other half, I run upstairs to my locker and grab my gun then head out front of the school as students are loading onto the different buses that take them to their neighborhood. I see the bus that reads Cherryhill on the display and head towards it, I spit to see if my mouth is still bleeding before I get on the bus. It was mostly saliva with a tiny bit of blood mixed in, I'm good.

When I got back to the hood nobody was on the block not even Robo. So I go up Robo's house and page my niggaz there all around Chardae's house they said the police on some bullshit so they left the block until 4 o'clock when police's shift changed so I walked around Chardae's. "Damn! What the fuck happen to your lip" Glenn says as we slap hands. "Shorty, you ain't goin believe this shit!" I say slapping hands wit all my niggaz sitting in the kitchen at the table or on the washing machine, or on a crate.

Anyway, I tell my niggaz about the lil rendezvous at the carryout and they tell me Bean shot Pelle Pelle last night.

Word has it he got hit four or five times but he's still in the hospital. "It would have been nice if yall let a nigga know yall burnt a nigga up, if them niggaz wasn't bluffin they coulda smoked me for real!" I say a lil upset.

"You wasn't strapped?" Bean asked.

"That ain't the point," I say mad that I wasn't strapped.

"Naw you right I feel you." Bean admits.

"I got some weed, I can't roll it my lip fucked up oh and what's up Chardae, Marie, and Nelly? I see yall got two new girls rolling wit yall, what's they names?"

"Ask them!" Chardae says.

"What's yall names?" Brit-Brit and Teaki they tell me, I sat around Chardae's for about an hour then left to go home. On my way home I go past Keyco's house and he's just getting in on his porch turning his key. "What's up? Why you ain't stop past the gym. I know Lil Stay High told you, I could look at ya eyes and tell you ran into that nigga. Fuck happen to your lip?" Keyco ask. I run the story down to him.

"Hell no!" He says.

"Hell yeah," I say back.

Beep Beep Beep

Beep Beep Beep

"I just left this nigga let me see the phone Keyco. What up?" I ask Glenn thru the phone.

"Yo when you come up the hill bring me one with you. Yo, I don't even know if I'm coming back out, my head hurt, im high, and my body tired. I'm around Keyco's come around here then we just going to walk around my house together." I tell him.

"Aight" he says and hangs up, Lil glenn shows up around Keyco's with Poka and Lil Greezy with him. We all stayed aournd Keyco's long enough for me to play Poka in a game of Madden that ended with me winning 50 dollars. My house is only about a five minute walk from Keyco's, we leave out to go to my house so I can grab the work for Glenn. But as were leaving out of Keyco's yard, "yo, did one of yall niggaz drop some money? Cuz it's a hundred dollar bill on my floor." Keyco says from his door.

"Damn, hell yeah that's mine's Keyco" Glenn says checking his pockets. "Well it ain't goin walk to you," Keyco says. Glenn go gets the hundred dollar bill from Keyco then we walk around my house and I give Glenn a ounce of crack and I give Poka and Greezy one also cuz I told them I don't think I'm coming back out tonight. I go in the houe and fall asleep for a few hours only to be waken up by, Beep! Beep! Beep!

Beep! Beep! Beep!

"Shut dat damn thing off and what the hell you need with a beeper anyway?" My granny says waking me up. I mumble something to my granny then call the number paging me.

"What's up, who this Keyco?" I ask thru the phone.

"Yeah he replies then says, "yo why ya man petty as shit, that hunnit dollars wasn't Glenns."

"Who's was it?" I ask.

"Jah's, he came in here and asked me did I see a hunnit dollar bill on the coffee table. It must of fell on the floor or whatever, but the point is that it wasn't Glenn's money and Jah mad as shit. He said can't nobody come in this mufucka unless it's you or T-Rod. He just left out he said he was goin to fuck Lil Glenn up for disrespecting him."

"Tell em I'll give em his money back an......."I tried to say hoping it would fix the situation but as I knew it wasn't about the money and Keyco confirmed my thought cutting me off saying, "You know Jah got money out his ass, he mad somebody would come in here an steal. You know he hates to be disrespected." Keyco tells me.

"You think he went up the wall to look for Glenn?" I ask.

"I don't know." Keyco says sounding a little depleted.

"Aight let me see if I can find this nigga "lenn before him and Jah bump heads." I say then hang up the phone.

(Me and Keyco like family, I known Keyco since elementary school. Shit, Keyco is the one that hooked me and Angie up. Not to mention that

Keyco and T-Rod are cousins and it always been love between us three. I don't know why Glenn would do some dumb shit like this. I heard Glenn was a petty nigga before he started hanging up The Wall but since he been hanging wit us he seemed to have changed. (I guess old habbits die hard.)

I called up Robo's nobody was in there, I called around Chardae's no Glenn. So I checked the time 8:51, it ain't that late so I paged Glenn and he ain't call back. Fuck it im goin outside, I grab my hoody and jacket then strap up about to leave when my father walks in.

"Where you off to kiddo?" He asks me.

"Outside, you see Lil Glenn out there in your travels?" I ask him.

"Yeah, that's why I'm coming to see where you was at."

"Why? What happen? Why was you comin to check on me?"

"Me and your mother was comin from out Westport seeing your lil brothers you know Jerrell (My brother, I'm the oldest he's next to the oldest!) is about to turn 13. He told us to tell you come see him but anyway we were looking for you and someone said yall was on Vick's porch so we get our ride to take us down there and we see some commotion. Glenn and Jah goin at it, Glenn tried to fight back but Jah got the best of em."

"What about Manna and em?"

"They ain't jump in it?"

"Where Was they?" I ask.

"They was up there but Jah had two of his goons up there with their hands in their waist. I heard he told Manna and them this didn't have nothing to do with them. This was between him and Glenn."

"Oh, yeah," I say.

"Yeah," he replies.

"Fuck it," I say taking off my jacket, what the fuck am I'm supposed to do I mumble to myself and go back and lay down.

CHAPTER 15'S INTRO

The week went by, then the weekend showed up and guess who showed up with it? "Big Sexy", I use to have a problem with his name too but it ain't no homo shit that's been his name for years plus he's a savage. I'm up the wall finishing up a pack and Big Greezy pulls up in his silver bubble Crown Vic with Big Sexy in the passenger seat. Now both of these niggaz older than me, im 17 at the time and Greezy's about 21 and Sexy's 22 I believe. These niggaz grew up together they pretty much watched us grow up for real. Sexy's about 6 feet 6 inches some shit like that, a tall skinny mufucka. Greezy's probably almost 6 feet but not quite skinny maybe a inch or two off. So they pull up blasting the Lox CD when I go to the car.

CHAPTER 15
If it ain't one thing

"What you about to do Scotty?" Greezy asked turning down the music. "Shit, I'm just out chere doin what I do you know, what's up sexy? When you come home today?" I ask.

"Naw they let me out last night, but I stayed in the crib."

"Get in Scotty, ride wit us!" Greezy says.

"Man, I can't ride wit yall, yall pretty boys two light skineed niggaz wit golds shinnin, I ain't goin to get no bitch's!" I say joking.

"Cut the bullshit get in nigga!" Sexy says.

"You dirty?" (Dirty= have anything illegal on you) Greezy askes me as im getting in the back seat of the car.

"I'm strapped, but I ain't got no drugs on me they in the stash." I say. "Look at you, I thought you was goin to be a basketball player now you turning out not to be shit just like the rest of us." Sexy says with a laugh.

"Where we goin at anyway?" I ask.

"Over East Baltimore to grab these pills," Greezy tells me.

"What kinda pills?" I ask.

"E pills," Greezy responds trying to read my eyes to see if I turn my nose up.

"E pills? Ecstacy?" I asked kinda sounding naive due to the fact I didn't know my nigga/niggaz popped E's.

"No Excedrine, Yeah Ecstacy!"

"I ain't know you be fuckin wit them pills Greezy, you fuckin wit em too sexy?" I ask.

"I'mma fuck wit em today," sexy responds then greezy begins to confess how he started poppin.

"Don't go runnin ya mouth about it but I was down Coppin Court wit Lydee last week, he put me on them bitch's. Them E's where it's at, I only pop on the weekend though." Greezy says as if that made it alright.

"How they make you feel?" I ask.

"Goddamn Great! I love em!" Greezy says.

"Danm they like that?" I asked.

"Yeah they like that."

We get over East Baltimore and they got cars lined up.

"These pills must be good, fuck it get me one Greezy. Do they got any weed up here?" I say giving greezy 20 dollars for a pill and fifty dollars for some weed.

"Here Scotty," Greezy says handing me a pill and a jar with about 15 maybe 20 dollars worth of weed in it.

"What the fuck is this?" I say holding up the jar.

"It's a fifty." Greezy says.

"A fifty, I repeat? CLICK CLACK, these niggaz just got over on you Greezy I got something for their ass," I say as I cock a bullet in the chamber of my gun then ask, "Which one of em gave you this weed?"

"Chill shorty what the fuck is you about to do?" Sexy asked.

"A nigga just burned Greezy for fifty dollars so imma bout ta burn they ass." I tell him.

"Ain't nobody burn me, that's purple. That's what a fifty of purple look like, two or three dutch's depend on how you roll em." Greezy says.

"Well why you ain't say that at first?"

"I thought you knew, the shit in a jar smell that shit." We stopped at a liquor store to get a 5th of Belevedere vodka, a cranberry juice, a water, and of course blunts. We all eat our pills as soon as we get back in the car.

"So where we goin to now?" I ask while breaking a blunt worth of weed up in a twenty dollar bill.

"We ready to hit the mall, I told sexy I was going to grab him a couple of things.' Greezy says

'How long this pill goin to take before I start to feel it?" I asked

(By the time we got to the mall I had put two cups of vodka & cranberry in me, a blunt of purple, and that E pill. Talk about high, I was in the mall telling bitch's I was a astronaut.)

'Hi I'm Neil, Neil Armstrong that is." I say to a group of bitch's in the mall.

"Oh my GOD ya breath stink, you smell like alcohol." One of the bitch's said.

"See no, See my breath doesn't stink, I just have expensive taste your just not familiar with the fragrance. That's a thirty dollar cup of liquor on my breath and you don't know nothin bout it." I respond in a voice close to a whisper.

"Man, come on Scotty leave these damn girls alone!" Greezy says ushering me away. I look back at the bitch's, "to infinity and beyond!" I say walking off.

"Yo, yall not high? I'm high as shit!" I say to Greezy and Sexy as we left the mall.

We both bought sexy a few things and we brought a few things for ourselves. (Back in the car)

"I ain't goin to lie, I never really liked Crown Vic's but this joint aight right here." I say in a whisper. "Feel the leather

Sexy that shit nice ain't it?"

"I'm tryin go to the strip club Sexy says gritting his teeth."

"It's only a quarter til eight" Greezy says.

"Who gives a fuck that bitch open and it's bitches in there Sexy says."
"I'm wit it, they goin let me in" I ask."

"We ain't taking no for an answer!" Sexy says lighting a cigarette.

I count the money I got on me and its 12 hunnit and some change. I already spend 3 and some change at the mall, all this money is from the ounce I sold today. I still had about 20 pills stashed on the block. "Man, you back there counting your money, yall up there jamming everyday. I know you ain't worried about know couple hunnit dollars," Greezy says. "Here sexy," I give him the 2 something and keep the stack. I only planned on spending 300 out of my stack. When we walk in the strip club it feels like I'm walking in slow motion, like I'm the slickest nigga in the world. Music bumpin lights flashing and bitch's everywhere half naked shaking to the 80 dimes nigga song. I don't know who was singing the hook but that shit was rocking. "Bal-ti-more we know how to party so put your drink down and let's get started."

"Baaal-ti-mooore".

"You tipping?" A brown skinned, long hair, about a hunnit and twenty five pound stripper wearing a burgundy thong asked me.

"I'm doin everything," I say twirling my head as she twirled her hips seductively.

"Is that right?" She ask.

"Yeah that's right."

"What you drinking Scotty?" Sexy ask me from the bar.

"Whatever, naw get me a shot of that shit we was drinking in the car." I tell Sexy.

"Ay, get her one too." After bein in the club for about five minutes I start to notice my surroundings and I notice ain't nobody in here forreal. It's two old heads that look like there pushin 50 and it's two niggaz about our age, well Sexy and them age. And it's about 10 strippers the whole time I'm thinking it's more people in here but I'm just noticing it's mirrors on all the walls so I counted everybody about four times.

"Man I'm trippin," I tell myself so I go in the bathroom to throw some water on my face to get a grip.

"You in here hidin from me? Huh Mr. I'm doin everything," the stripper says walking in the bathroom.

"Hiding? Sorry I don't know the meaning of that word." I say to the stripper while I'm in the mirror stretching and rubbing my face.

"Oh well I guess you just like women to chase you then, is that it? Are you alright?" She asked.

I guess she just notices how I'm geekin in the mirror.

'Yeah, I'm fine. My bad I just left you by yourself out there, come on we can go back out there, im good!" I say stepping towards the door.

"Or we could stay in here for a minute" she says putting her hand on the door stopping me from opening it.

"Don't tell me you scared to be alone with me Mr. Everything" she says licking her lips showing her tongue ring.

"Umm.......... I, im........" (I ain't know what to say to this bitch, this my first time at the strip club. Lucky she was a professional.)

"Why you looking at my tongue ring like that? You shouldn't stare at things if you can't afford em," she says running her tongue across her teeth.

"How much?" I asked still staring.

"Since your cute, Ahhhh hundred dollars," she said and smiled the most beautiful smile or maybe it was the liquor and pill.

I stuck my hand in my pocket as she pushed the button in on the middle of the door knob locking the bathroom door. "I gave her two fifty dollar bills and she put them in her bra. I put the rest of my money in my pocket and she unbuttoned my pants. I started to pull my pants down with my hand that was in my pocket and she started to help me. I had almost forgot until I looked down that I had on my Tommy Hilfiger underwear that Angie had brought me. It made me think about her until the stripper grabbed my ..attention through my boxers stroking it until it got hard, then she fanagled it out of the split in my boxers as I leaned my back against the door. She leans down and grabs me by the waist to balance herself playfully licking up and down the length of my shaft twirling her tongue and tongue ring around the rim of my head when she got to the top of the shaft. "Umm, Um, Um," I repeat rolling my head in counter clockwise circles with my eyes closed.

"Um um, are you okay?" She asked taking her mouth off of me and stroking with her hand.

"Um, um, yup" I say still rolling my head with my eyes closed.

"Sit on the sink, my legs are cramping." She says.

"Can you hand me my cigarettes out my pocket while your down there and my lighter too? It should be in my back pocket." Why are you whispering she asked as she digs through my pockets?

(I sat on the sink and lit my cigarette and she goes back to work.)

"Suck it slow," I tell her as I lightly begin to rub my hand thru her hair. She obliges slowly going up and down with her lips pucked, artfully going from sucking to licking and back to sucking as I rock the top half of my body back and forth.

"Ummhmm," I say then take another hit off my cigarette.

"Boy, put that damn cigarette out your smoking the filter, what's the matter with you? You got one of them pills in you, don't you?"

"Um, how you know?" I ask.

"You funny as shit, I know you wanna fuck!" She says grabbing my dick tight squeezing it to get my attention. My eyes pop open shocked from the sudden amount of slight pain, and I'm bout to cuss this bitch out but she was just staring at me. Looking like Pocahontas with my dick in her hand.

"I know you wanna fuck, and my pussy's wet as shit," she says then sticks her free hand into her panties moaning seductively as she plays with herself. I eased down off the sink and grabbed her ass and let my hand slide down her ass cheek until it got to her warm, wet, split.

"How old are you anyway?" She asked rubbing my rock hard dick up against her panties.

"I'm old enough!"

"So are you gonna fuck me or am I just going to stand here with your dick in my hand?" She says with a smile then licks the outline of my ear. I take one leg out of my jeans then spin Pocahontas around and bend her over the sink.

"You know this is going to be another hunn..Uhh, umm!" she starts to moan as I give her long slow strokes from the back. It felt like my dick was vibrating as I gave it to her passive aggressively from behind, getting up under her with every stroke.

"You..uhh you about to make me cum," she moans so I start to give it to her a little harder, a little deeper as her leg begins to tremble. We come out of the bathroom and sexy is on the stage with three strippers. He got every bit of two to three hundred ones in his hand periodically making it drizzle about 20-25 ones at a time it's already a nice amount of bills on the stage. He motions his arm for me to join him but I wave em off and go sit in the back and wait for Pocahontas to come from freshening up. It was about 10 o'clock when we left the strip club. A few people had paged me but wasn't none of them 911 so I didn't press myself to call nobody back. So we were in the car headed back to the hood.

"Yo, so what you saying just cause she a stripper I can't make her my girl?" I ask in the car on the way back from the club.

"Yo you really serious," Sexy says.

"So what a stripper can't have a boyfriend?" I ask.

"Don't let him drink out that bottle sexy, he sucked that bitch off in that bathroom," Greezy says.

"Look I'm not telling you what and what not to do Scotty but that bitch probably fuck a different nigga every night!" Sexy tells me.

"You heard what Styles P said.

"Regardless who she fuck I'm the nigga she deserve." I say in my defense.

"But he wasn't talking bout no fuckin stripper Scotty!" Greezy says.

"Aight, but what if I love her though?"

"AHH Ha Ha Ha AHHHH Haa Ha!" Sexy and Greezy both bust out laughing. When we pulled up on the block Glenn and Poka was on their way to Robo's house. (So were we)

"Where y'all bout to go?" Greezy asked Poka and Glenn through the car window.

"Up Robo's." Poka responds.

"We coming up there I'm about to park in the lot." Greezy says.

"Yo take me down the gas station real quick Greezy?" Lil Glenn asked. "Get in," Greezy tells him.

"Let me out, im going up Robo's I need to use the phone." I say opening the car door.

"You want this gun Glenn?" I ask lifting my shirt up as I stood outside of the car.

"They ain't stop making guns when they made yours," he tells me and lifts his shirt up to expose his gun handle.

Me and Poka walk up Robo's and Glenn, Sexy, and Greezy ride to the gas station.

Roll this up Poka, I say throwing him the jar of purple and goin to grab the phone off of the counter.

"Umph, umph, cough! Damn what this is Scotty?" Poka asked choking off the weed.

"That's that purple, that Barney nigga." I tell him.

"What y'all took Sexy to get some clothes and shit?"

"Yeah," I respond as I sat on the couch, grab the phone and start dialing.

About 5 minutes later Sexy and them come banging on the door.

"Fuck y'all banging like that for?" Poka says opening the door.

"Man, I'm goin back to jail, it's a camera down that bitch!" Sexy says. "I don't know, I think the camera just watch the pumps and inside the store he got hit outside the store and away from the pumps." Greezy says.

"I leave y'all for 5 minutes, what the fuck happened?" I ask.

"Click Click stupid ass gun jammed," Glenn say jerking the slide of his gun.

"Yo what the fuck is that, where the fuck you get that from a antique gun store?" I say to Glenn.

"Man, fuck you! It's a German Rugger, (click click) a fiend sold it to me," Glenn says cocking the jammed bullet out of the chamber.

"Where that bullet fall at?"

"Here," I say picking up the bullet.

"Let me see it!" Sexy says.

"No wonder it jammed you got 9mm bullets in here."

"It's a 9 though," Glenn says.

"It's a 9 Rugger, not a 9 millimeter! You gotta put Rugger bullets in here or its goin keep jamming." Sexy tells Glenn.

"Yeah yeah fuck all that, who did y'all shoot?" I ask.

"That nigga Jah tried to bitch me, I ain't know he was behind me and that nigga reached around me and grabbed my money out of the window while I was paying for my shit." Glenn says.

"I thought that nigga was just playin until i saw Glenn whip out," Sexy adds in.

"What I do when he came out that gas station tho?"

"You was bluffing nigga!"

"I ain't wanna hit Keyco!"

"Ain't nobody tell you snatch the gun from me." Glenn says.

"Keyco was down there, yo what the fuck type games yall playin yo? Yo y'all niggaz geekin!" I say.

"We geekin! Yo shouldn't have never took my money out of that window. He should of let that shit go after we fought," Glenn says.

"So y'all shot Keyco's stepfather?"

What the fuck, I say to myself.

CHAPTER 16'S INTRO

Three days after the shooting at the gas station Jah came of out the hospital. I hadn't seen Keyco since Jah got shot. I called him once and he immediately told me he was going to call me right back, but he never called back. I didn't know how to take that. I know he did that before. I've done it plenty of times to people. Not intentionally but I just forgot to call back, but considering what was going on like I said I didn't know how to take it, so I didn't call again. I went to see Tyrod to see how he felt about the situation. He hasn't been on the block as much because he found a lil nigga near his house to give pills to. He was paying the lil nigga next to nothing so he was content. I went to see T-rod he was strapped. I was strapped. It seemed like so much was goin on niggaz couldn't rest. We use to have an inner peace but now it's seems like everybody is a little on edge. Me and T-rod kicked it for an hour or two in his crib smoking and tripping. I let him know about my E-pill/strip club experience. He let me know he was paying his worker $50 dollars a night and giving him a few bags of weed and food from the carry-out. He said the lil nigga was only 13, What he need a bunch of money for. I told him I ain't really know how I felt about the situation with Jah, then the weed gave us a crazy idea. Let's walk up there and see what's up with the nigga Jah.

CHAPTER 16
Forget about it

"Come in," Keyco says after not fully opening the door for about 5 seconds that seemed like 50 as we stared at each other.

"I thought you were ready to shut the door in our face." T-Rod says slapping hands with Keyco.

"Why would I do that?" Kecyo responds looking confused then says, "I called you back yesterday to Scotty. Your grandmother said you had left out. Me and Jah was just talking about y'all niggaz." Keyco finished.

"Yeah, me and T-Rod was just talking about ya..AAw" my sentence breaking as I saw a gun's muzzle turning the corner from keyco's kitchen to his living room.

"Good job Keyco, up against the wall bumbaclatts!" Jah says stepping out of the kitchen shirtless with a bandaged shoulder and what looks like a Uzi in his hands talkin shit in his jamaican accent.

"Wut ya tauwt (thought) ya catch me laid up in bed and finish me, try again mudafucka's!"

"Jah ain't nobody.." was all I got out before he cut me off.

"I ain't trine hear dat shit, which wanna you rude boys should I give it to first huh?" Jah says waving the Uzi back and forth from me to T-Rod. "Keyco make sure Ty-Rod stays put, C'mon to da basement Scotty I don't wanna get blood on the carpet."

"So this what it is Jah?" I say looking him square in the eyes.

"Just come on! take your bullet like a man." He reply's.

"Aight," I say and take a step forward.

"Ahh! ha! ha! ha! Pussyboy was gonna walk downstairs and let me kill him. I had em goin didn't I? So this is what it is Jah?" He says laughing repeating me.

"'Ha, ha," I say whipping out my 380 as soon as Jah puts the Uzi in his waistband.

"Okay Okay respect, maybe you wasn't goin out easy as I tauwt (thought)."

"Yeah I was goin to let somebody have it, but naw on some real shit, how's the shoulder?" I ask putting my gun back in my waist.

"It's alright, a little sore, but alright." Jah says.

"Look man, Imma come clean wit you. So you know where I stand on the situation, cuz ain't no secret it's a complicated situation for me." I say. First off I knew Keyco since forever, me and shorty like family. My niggaz is my niggaz, I love them and I ain't goin to sit by and watch no harm get done to em. I say that to say this, I could never do nothing to hurt Keyco and I know how he feel about you. So that goes without saying but imma say it. You ain't gotta worry about me but if any of your goons come at my niggaz I don't owe them no love, loyalty, or none of dat. I hate this whole situation for real, but shit, it is what it is, you know?"

"Yeah, yeah I know it's fucked up you got shiesty mudafucka's so close to you, your a good kid and I respect your honesty so I'm not gonna add on or take from it, but I will give you some words of advice. There is no honor amongst thieves. If he will come into a house that you invited him into and steal you know wit forget about it, no bad blood between us." Jah says.

"That's real good to hear." I say.

"Nuff bout me, Keyco told me some guys tried to carve you up at school." "Aw them bluffing ass niggaz, now that you mention it I should go pay them chumps a visit." I say.

"Ay man, you gotta take it easy out here, matter fact I got a book I want you to look at." Jah tells me.

We sat in Keyco house and smoked two bones of that Jamacian green. Jah gave me a book, 48 laws of power. (I know a lot of niggaz refer to 48 laws of power in their books, raps, or whatever but I was reading the shit in 01. I just don't want y'all think I'm copying off them niggaz) Anyway we smoked he gave me the book then I went in the house.

When I got in the door of my house I was overwhelmed by the smell of my grandmother's fried chicken.

"Umm it smell good in here, KFC ain't got nothing on you granny." I say walking thru the kitchen.

"Whatever boy, Chic looking for you" my grandmother tells me.

"Well here I am, in the flesh." I say jokingly then add, "Naw where's my favorite cousin? I ain't see her car our front!"

"She upstairs on the phone, Greg (Greg: my uncle) has her car getting someone to check her breaks, tell her that her food is ready when you go upstairs." My grandmother yells as im headed up the stairs.   "What up Chic, I heard you were looking for me," I say peeking my head in my grandmother's room. She sticks her index finger up indicating for me to hold on so I go into my room and pull out my bottom drawer and lift up the false bottom and put my 380 in the flat space and grabbed my money and begin counting it. 20, 40, 60, 80, 17, 20, 40, 60, 80, 18, 20, 40, 60..

"Jamal," Chic says peeking in my room.

"What up cuz?" I ask then tell her to come in.

"I was riding past The Wall before I came down here and it was about 5 police cars up there they had everybody sitting on the ground. So I got out the car cuz I thought you were up there." Chic says.

"Did they let em go?" I asked then mumble to myself more so, "they allways harassing mufucka's."

"They let everybody go except for Manna, they said he threw a gun." "They said he threw a gun, did they find it?" I asked.

"Yeah, they had a gun," she said.

"You sure it wasn't their own gun?" I ask.

"Naw, they had put it in a plastic bag."

"Shit! If it ain't one thing it's a mufuckin nother. What's wrong wit cha breaks though?" I ask changing the subject.

"I don't know they squeaking, that shit sounds a mess. I was looking for your father so he could look at em for me."

"Yeah, ain't no telling where that nigga at." I say then look at my money.

"What I messed up your count? Why you got all your money layin on that bed anyway, what you about to take me shopping?"

"Girl, by the time we get to the mall it would be about to close and we both know you shop for hours."

"Yeah, I guess we can just go tomorrow." She says.

"Real smooth chic, how you just talked yaself into that! Granny said the food ready."

"Well put that money up, come on let's eat."

"Aight, here."

"What's this for?"

"Your breaks."

"Aww, thank you."

"Forget about it." I say in my best Goodfella impersonation.

CHAPTER 17'S INTRO

It's been about a month since manna got locked up. They sent him to some juvenile joint for the gun. I talked to his aunt she said he should be home for Christmas they want him to do at least 6 to 9 months and today is April 5th 3 days before my birthday. The blocks been so-so it's not as much money coming thru. I think it's for a few reason. It could be fiends are a little scared to come up here and cop (buy) at night because some bitch niggaz came up here and took some pop-shots at us. A fiend got shot in the process so I guess there a little more cautious. Police have been putting a lil more heat on us since the fiend got shot. The streets talk so the police know we shot pelle pelle and Jah. They just didn't have any witnesses so it wasn't shit they could do without Jah or pelle pelle co-operating with them. Not to metion O and Row still being locked up for that murder. Their trial is set for the first of June. Then reems cooking skills ain't like "O's" so this batch of coke ain't as good as the one's O cooked but it's still aight. And reem..well reem is reem even though him and O are brothers their like night and day in some area's. Reem that's my nigga though with his Jermaine Dupree looking ass. Anyway I've been spending more and more time with big greasy and sexy.Me and lil glenn we've been popping pills all month fucking with them niggaz. The niggaz two doors away from tyrod's house starting selling E's the nigga Delroy and tommy/tom-E.

Del (Delroy) and tommy I swear they like two of the coolest niggaz in the world. They ain't with all that gun bustin shit them niggaz just like to have a good time. So here I am 3 days before my birthday and I'm in the house looking through this book Jah gave me. "Law #22 us the surrender tactic" to disarm your enemy. Law #15 "destroy your enemy completely". I wonder is that why he ain't bring no kickback yet. If this nigga study this book and do this shit. He probably got something serious he's planning for the wall boys, but why give me the book that goes against Law #3 "Conceal your intentions." I don't know what kind of shit he on but..beep! beep! beep! beep! beep! beep! I check my pager- tyrod, let me call and see what he's hollering about.

CHAPTER 17
Hand in the cookie jar!

"What it is my nigga?" I say to T-Rod thru the phone.

"Yo, this nigga Reem losing his mind or something, I don't know if he started smoking weed or what but he need to get his self together."

"Slow down pimpin, what happen?" I ask.

"Reem bought me a ounce down here the other night and instead of waiting til I sell the ounce to pay him, I gave him the money up front. Now he talking about I ain't never give him no money."

"That's crazy!" I say.

"I know right, what the fuck I look like playing games about some petty as ounce. My lil nigga selling damn near a ounce a day."

"Yeah, that's crazy, im ready to walk down there. Is Del or Tommy out front?"

"Boy you terrible, them pills got you by da balls."

"Man, I'm on my way down there!" I say then hang up the phone.

Tyrods house is about a 7 minute walk from my house. The weathers been nice the last couple of days, so I get on Tyrods block and I see Tyrod on Dels front porch. Del is sitting on a milk crate with some girl braiding his hair.

"What's up Rod, what's up Del?" I say slapping hands with them.

"Where that nigga Tom-E at?" I ask.

"He in the house, matter of fact go in there and get that blunt from the nigga," Del says to me with his head tilted as the girl braids.

"What's up Tom-E Guns my nigga, fuck you in here cooking?"

"You know doin my spaghetti thing, nothin to heavy. What brings you down here?" Tommy asks tasting the spaghetti sauce.

"I just came to holler at you niggaz, but since I'm here where the pills at?"

"Scotty 2 Hotty, it ain't the weekend what you changed ya scheduled?" "Naw, my birthday in three days and y'all niggaz be runnin out of pills so I'm just getting mine's now."

"Run out, man we just re'd up, new joints you ever had the stars?"

"Naw, y'all ain't got the cash money joints no more?"

"Fuck them cash money's, these stars where it's at. I took one yesterday I ain't been to sleep yet."

"Did you get some pussy wit the star in you though?"

"Man, I couldn't nut, the bitch sucked me off, I fucked her, she sucked me off again I started fucking her again then just said fuck it. The bitch thought something was wrong, I think she thought her pussy was bullshit."

"Hell no," I say smiling jus thinking about the drugs.

"Stars," Tommy says nodding his head in approval.

"Let me get 3 for fifty," I say grabbing the half smoked blunt out of the ashtray lighting it. "Oh, Del sent me in here to get this too." I say as I walk out of the kitchen.

"Whole up, I'm right behind you 2 hotty. So what you doin on ya B-day?" Tommy ask as we're walking out on the porch.

"My son is about to turn 18 ain't you?" T-Rod says.

"You betta believe it." I say sounding like Gary Coleman.

"So where we at? Ya shit on a Saturday too!" Tyrod says.

"I'm thinking bout partying from Thursday to Sunday, fuck it why not. I got to much shit to do to try and do it all in one day. My stripper bitch wanna do something, my niggaz, you know we goin do something. My girl wanna do something, my cousin Chic said she was taking me out to eat, my teacher even told me to make sure I come to school on Friday!" "The sexy one, Miss Fills?" Tyrod ask.

"Yeah Ms. Fields not Fills dummy." I say.

"He get real defensive about his teacher you see him," Tyrod says to Del and Tommy.

"Fuck that, did you notice the first person he mention doin something with wasn't his girl, wasn't his niggaz, wasn't even his cousin, but his stripper bitch." Del says putting me on blast.

"Man y'all trippin, T-rod you popping one of these Jiffy's with me?" I say shaking the three E-pills in my hand.

"Damn how many pills you buy?" T-rod ask. "Not enough, my stripper said she goin take one with me." I tell them.

"Yo, I gotta meet this stripper," Tyrod says.

"For what?" I ask.

"So I can find out who got my man head in the clouds."

"Yeah aight, I'm goin up The Wall and hustle, I gotta make some money I've been bullshitting these last couple of days." I say as I slap hands with everybody then walk off the porch.

———

When I get up The Wall Bean is up there talking to some girls, the girls are in a car and Bean is standing at the curb. I slap hands with him and tell him I'm dirty so I keep it pushing, Poka is sitting on The Wall smoking a blunt, so I ask him is it hot (hot:police activity) up here. "Naw, shit cool" he tells me. So I walk to the stash spot and stash my cracks and my 3 E-pills. Walking back from my stash I see Lil Greezy headed towards Robo's.

"Where you ready go at?" I ask Lil Greezy, up Robo's right quick." He responds.

"Here take this up there and put it somewhere for me." I say handing him my gun.

"Smoke wit me, like you joke wit me" I say walking over to Poka.

"Come here Scotty!" Bean says from the curb.

"What's up?" I ask when I get up there.

"Reem looking for you," Bean informs me.

"Yeah, I ain't surprised, who your friends?" I say referring to the girls sitting in the car.

"Shimmy and Sheeky," Bean tells me.

"What up y'all," I say peeking in the car to get a better look at the two red bones. They were cute but I ain't really know what to say so I got outta there.

"Can a nigga smoke wit you Poka?" I say walking away from the car.

"You the one over there brown nosing wit Bean."

"Here I go right here baby how many you want?" Poka yells to a fiend. "Give me 5 I got 46, I had to get some cigarettes. Ay if y'all know anybody trying to rent a room let me know my name is Rose."

"How much you renting it for?" I ask.

"Two fifty a month." She tells me.

" What if I only need it for a day or two?" I ask.

"I don't know, 25 dollars a night or something like that."

"You ain't got know roaches running around in that mufucka?"

"Boy, all I do is clean, I ain't got no damn roaches or mice, my floor is clean enough to eat off off."

"Ay we might could do some business baby," I say.

"Here you go mama," Poka says handing her the five pills.

"What the fuck you looking at me like that for?" I ask Poka.

"Yo, what you trying freak that lady? You a nasty nigga, Big grezzy told me you sucked that stripper bitch pussy now you freaking crackheads." Poka says.

"Man shut the fuck up, ain't nobody trying to freak that lady, I got a feeling it's goin to be a wild weekend imma need somewhere to take my bitch's."

"Scotty! Glenn and em want you! Him, my brother, and Sexy up Robo's wit dem pills in em." Lil Grezzy tells me as he comes around the corner. I go grab my E pills from out of my stash then go upstairs to Robo's.

"Yo, y'all high as shit," I say looking at Glenn, Sexy and Big Greezy sitting in a semi circle at the kitchen table. It's the usual setting, on the table is two open packs of cigarettes my 380, a 44 bulldog, a partially drunken 5th of liquor with plastic cups filled with alcohol in front of everybody sitting at the table. Glenn smoking a blunt, Sexy and Big Grezzy both have cigarettes lit.

"They been at that table for 3 hours Scotty." Robo tells me.

"Well if you can't beat em join em," I say eating one of my pills and pulling up a chair to the table. I sat up Robo's til damn near eleven o'clock then went in the house still high, I don't smoke in my house. I'm pretty sure my grandmother knows I smoke but I never smoked in front of her. So when I get in I set down stairs on the phone for about 2 hours of talkin my girls head off then I got the urge to smoke so I went in the bathroom like I was about to take a shower and cut the water on as hot as it goes, then stuffed a towel under the door then set on the edge of the tub for two hours talking to my stripper bitch chain smoking weed and cigarettes. Then I got a brilliant idea, my granny's liquor stash. I could take a cup without her knowing. It's not like im stealing, im just borrowing a cup out of her fifth. So I shut the bathroom door behind me and head down-stairs looking for the Bacardi, first I check all the lower cabinets,(nothing) maybe she put it in the upper cabinets so my lil cousins can't get to it (nope)! "Shit nothing!" I say as I rampage thru the fridge, then out of the corner of my eye the pantry of course. After a brief search of the pantry I find the bottle on the top shelf in the pantry, so I turn around to set it on the table to pour a cup. "Caught, with your hand in the cookie jar!" My grandmother says standing behind me with her arms folded.

"Oh shi...you scared the mess out of me." I say to my grandmother.

"No wonder they want a conference with me at the school, you a 'al-key' (alkey:alcholic).

"It ain't even like that," I say.

"Well how is it? You in the bathroom smoking weed then you come down here to grab a shot of liquor. That's how it looks to me!"

"Yeah, well maybe it is like that."

"Have ya ass ready for school in the morning," she says and puts her bottle back.

CHAPTER 18'S INTRO

The next morning felt a little stranger after granny caught me dipping into her stash. I don't know if it was that or staying awake all night but something has me kinda jumpy. My grandfather works at a construction sight and he was grumpy because he had to take off work to take us to the school. The ride to the school was quiet with the exception to my grandfather's few sarcastic comments. "Do you want me to stop at the bar? so you can a get lil "nip" to take the edge off" or "roll us up a joint, shit I ain't going to work today." I wasn't in the mood for his shit, so I just stayed quiet and reclined in the back of the van until we got there. We had to be there before school started or before 1st period rather which started at 8:45 we pulled up a little before eight. My grandfather said he was going to wait in the van then he told me to give him enough weed to roll a few joints while he waited. He act like he was just joking but I think he wanted some weed for real.

CHAPTER 18
Im in love with a stripper!

"Thanks for coming Mrs. Ray, and I'm sorry for having you to have to come up here so early but please have a seat," Ms. Fields tells my granny. "I'm up in the morning anyway so it's no trouble really." My granny responds.

"Okay well let me get straight to the point, as of lately Jamal's attendance has been slipping at a rapid pace, he know's the work and he score's high when he's here but the grade's he's missing are going to cause him to fail and I'm hoping we can prevent that as we approach the end of this school year.

"Score's high," I bet my grandfather would have got a kick out of that one I think to myself as they go on about me.

"Well he leaves the house every morning and heads in the direction of the bus stop, I had know idea he was skipping and.." (Blah blah blah..)

They went on for close to a half hour then I walked my granny back to my grandfather's van. Students were standing around outside waiting for the bell to ring. I hollered at a few people until I saw Angie, I went and kicked it with her until the bell rung. She told me to stay in school all day and not to get on the bus after school, just meet her out front. So 3 o'clock rolls around and I'm standing out front with a Macy's bag in my hand when I hear.

"So what you got in the bag buster?" Angie says grabbing it out of my hand.

"Go head make me snuff you in front of the whole school." I tell her. "This came from another bitch cuz I know ain't no nigga buy you no pants and a belt." Angie says handing me the bag back.

"Ms. Fields got that for me so don't be calling her no bitch and why ain't we getting on the bus, you trying to set me up or something?"

"Boy please, my mother is taking us to dinner for your birthday and É.." (Honk Honk Honk)

"There she goes right there, come on."

"How you doin Miss. V?" I ask getting into the back seat of her volvo. "I'm doin just fine Happy Birthday mister, who went to Macy's?" Miss V asked.

"Thank you Miss. V and this just a lil gift my teacher got for me." I say smiling at Angie.

"Oh well that was nice, what did she get you?" Miss V asked.

"Some Calvin Klein pants and Calvin Klein belt."

"And he better not wear that shit around me!" Angie says.

"Now really stop it Angie your just being childish."

"Don't tell her nothing Miss. V, she don't run nothing. I'll throw my CK's on right now ain't nobody worried about her fake kurking." This is pretty much how our evening went. Ms. V treated us to a meal from the Cheesecake Factory. At the table Angie gave me my gift, a Kenneth Cole watch and it was classy. I told her it would go perfect with my CK hook-up. All in all we had a nice time Miss Vanessa told me I could spend the night with them if me and my teacher didn't already have plans. Everybodys a comedian I thought to myself.

"Where do you want me to drop you off at?" Miss V asked as we entered our neighborhood.

"Um, im goin to holler at Tyrod so I can pretty much walk from your house."

"When are you and Angie going to get your license?" Ms. V asked.

"I don't know, I don't really leave Cherryhill to much so I ain't never really..I mean I could drive though. I've been driving for years." I stutterded my response.

"Well I will bring y'all a book and y'all can study on your free time. Summer is coming maybe I'll let y'all take the car to 6 Flags or the beach or something." Ms. V says pulling in her parking spot.

Ain't this bout a bitch, I think to myself as I'm getting out of the car and see Pelle Pelle sitting in the playground behind Angie's house with his entourage.

"Ay y'all hurry up," I say to Angie and her mother as Pelle Pelle taps one of his friends and points to me.

"What's the matter?" Ms. V says glancing at all the guys in the playground. "You know them or something?"

"Something like that y'all just hurry up, walk faster!" I demand as they head towards their house while I stay put in the parking lot watching the playground.

"You coming in?" Angie asks as she stands on the porch with the door open.

"Naw just go in there and lock the door and don't open it. I will call you in a minute." I say as two of Pelle Pelle's home boys start to walk across the playground.

"You sure you don't wanna come in?" Angie says with a pleading look in her eyes.

"Just shut the damn door and lock it!" I say glancing back at the 2 niggaz coming my way. Soon as Angie's door shut I took off full speed in the opposite direction of Pelle Pelle's entourage. About 5 seconds after that POP! POP! POP! POP! Plinga-linga-ling! A car window shatters behind me I lowered my head and picked up speed grabbing a fence for balance as I turned the corner barley slowing down. POP! POP! "Ping!" a bullet ricochets off of the fence. I picked up speed again not far from T-Rods house.

"Hump, hump, hump," I pant as I get to Tyrods porch and see him standing in the door way with his gun in hand.

"Shorty," I say out of breath sliding past him "hump hump."

"Who the fuck you just shot nigga?" Tyrod says as he shuts and locks his door.

"You see any blood?" I ask T-Rod while I'm checking my arms and torso. "I feel funny like I got hit. Let me..Let me..let me hit that blunt." I say trying to catch my breath.

"A nigga was trying to shoot you?" Tyrod asked looking surprised then asking, "Where the fuck ya gun at?"

"I left it in the house." I say grabbing the blunt from T-Rod.

"I was wit my grandmother this morning then I was with Angie and her mother."

"So what the fuck happened, who was just shooting?"

"I don't know for sure, one of, well two of Pelle Pelle's homeboys chased me when I got out of Angie mother's car."

"They popped on you in front of Ms. Vanessa and Angie?"

"Naw I made them go in the house, then I tried to make a run for it."
"You should of went in Angie's house and called me!"

"Shoulda, woulda, I got away shit that's good enough for me, for now anyway. Matter of fact let me call Angie and let her know I'm alright."

Beep! Beep! Beep! My pager went off making me flinch, I guess I still was a lil edgy after bein shot at.

"This is probably her right here I say checking my pager, "aw shit this is my stripper where the phone at T-Riggy?" (No, I didn't call my stripper before I called my girl.) I called Angie and let her and her mother know I was alright. Then I called my stripper and she told me she got a room with a Jacuzzi at the Econo Hotel and Lounge, she would be out here to pick me up at 8:30. I looked at my Kenneth Cole it was 6:07, "Aight if you have any problems finding me call this number," I tell her before I hang up. I took a shower down Tyrod's and threw on my blue Calvin Klein dress jeans with my black CK belt. I took one of Tyrods black tank tops, threw on some of Tyrods degree, then grabbed my watch and strapped it back on. I looked out Tyrods window and saw everybody on Delroy's front, Del, Tommy, T-Rod, Sexy, Big Greezy, and Lil Glenn. There a few bitch's so I went out there after putting on my black Rockports. "Yo y'all niggaz terrible, yall stay getting high with out me." I say coming out of Tyrod's house.

"Ay theres my nigga right there, we was just taking bout ya crazy ass." Sexy says.

"I hope y'all was asking yaself how many pills y'all was getting me for my birthday."

"Ain't nobody buying you no pills, Tyrod just told us what you bout to do." Glenn says slapping hands with me.

"Um hmm you shinnin shorty," Grezzy says grabbing my wrist getting a better look at my watch.

"Crazy part is, I ain't buy nothin I got on, not even this tank top." "Yo, who pop'd on you and ya girl?" Sexy asked.

"I can't really say, I mean I'll know em if I see em but that nigga Pelle Pelle put the hit out, his bitch ass gotta go. Y'all trying ride back thru there?" Glenn asked.

"I just talked to my girl she said them niggaz ain't out there."

We kicked it on Del front, everybody put a pill in them all the niggaz anyway. Del gave me a free pill, I still had 2 stashed from the other day but anyway we stayed out there tripping until my stripper came and got me. I made her get out and come and meet my niggaz, plus I wanted to show her off. If you think she sexy with her clothes off you should of saw her with clothes on, stripper or no stripper I think I love her. But she came then we left, my niggaz stayed out front Dels.

CHAPTER 19'S INTRO

After a wild night which never ended it seemed like to me, the night took a few time-outs like when I dozed off in the jacuzzi or my lil nap I took while she gave me a massage but I still wouldn't classify either one of these as going to sleep. Anyway the next morning we took a shower together and I guess my stripper might of been use to doing this kinda thing cuz she had her overnight bag with fresh underwear and shit like that. So I sent her to the store to get me a pack of boxers and a toothbrush and a few other "nick nacks" while I rolled up a blunt of kind bud. Here I am sitting in the room in my boxers lighting my blunt with a stupid grin on my face, I see when I look up at the mirror. I guess I was grinning because I was thinking about last night's escapade's or maybe this morning's shower sex either way even when my mouth wasn't grinning my body was grinning don't ask me to explain how your body grins cuz I don't know, but that's what it felt like it was doing. So I light up my blunt and grab the remote and flip channels and stop on the news.

CHAPTER 19
Happy Birthday Nigga!

"We're here live on the scene in Cherry-Hill bringing you a morning up-date on last-nights gruesome, gruesome murders. I have with me South Baltimore's Police Chief and he's going to let us know as much as he can. Chief."

"Well right now all we really can tell you is the basic's. Last night around 11:50 pm there were a group of approximately 8 to 10 males sit-ting, standing, or what have you in the playground behind us when. As we were informed a car pulled up in the parking lot here to our left. We were told that the car backed all the way up to the dumpsters which hid it from out of view of the playground. As we're told two males with mask on exited the vehicle one of the masked gunmen were armed with an assault riffle and he begun firing into the crowd on the playground. Some of the members on the playground ran at this time and some fell from shots or just tripping over each other in the commotion. We were told that the second gunmen stood over any of the males that fell and fired execution styled shots into the fallen males heads. As of now we're still combing the scene for clues and shell cases. We have officers knocking on every door that has a view of the playground or parking lot. As of now we have 3 men dead, with another 3 shot we can't release any names as of now we're try-ing to locate family members and guys who were on the playground and got away unharmed. We're asking them to report to Southern district or call this number.."

"Alright, well thanks for your time Chief and we'll have a full update at 12, back to you Matt."

Wow, I say to myself as I hit the blunt, Police are going to be going crazy out that bitch. I started to call Angie but I didn't want it to show up on her caller ID that I'm calling her from a hotel, bad enough I ain't answer her pages last night.

"I got you a large boxers since you forgot to tell me what size you wear genius," my stripper says coming back in the room.

"Yeah I can fit a large only because my waist is small, you know that thing below my waist is a 3x at least."

"Your cute and funny," she says throwing the bag on the bed next to me. "You gotta work tonight?" I asked.

"I'm suppose to why you coming by the club?"

"Maybe, the niggaz I introduced you to last night was talking about it." "Well I need to get some sleep if imma work tonight."

"You ain't the only one, I been woke for two days for real. What time we gotta give the room up, at twelve?" I asked already knowing the answer. "Yeah, we got it for another 5 hours."

"Well I'm ready to sleep until 11:30 or are you tryin to get out of here?"

"Naw, we can sleep," we showered then slept until the cleaning lady came and woke us up.

"Oh I'm sorry I thought you would be gone by now."

"Sure you did peeking Tammy." Anyway she dropped me off up The Wall. I went up Robo's and as I'm coming in guess who's coming out, Glenn and Jennifer.

"Where you goin Glenn?" I asked.

"No where imma walk her downstairs right quick."

"What's up Jennifer?" I say as they start down the steps.

"Yo, you watch the news this morning?" I asked Glenn when he came back in Robo's.

"Nigga I am the news this morning," he tells me.

"Yeah, I kinda figured that was y'all niggaz, where everybody at?"

"Sexy on his way out here, he went uptown last night to swap those guns out." Glenn told me then asked, "You got some weed Scotty?"

"Yeah I still got a couple of bags from last night, I still got a pill too."

"What cha stripper ain't pop wit you?"

128

"Yeah she popped, Del had gave me a pill and I still had the one's for me and her. What's up with you and Jennifer though?"

"Shit, you know me and shorty use to fuck wit each other a few years ago, why, wut up?"

"Nuffin, just asking," I say dryly only to get a look from Glenn as if I was holding something back.

So me and Glenn bullshitted up Robo's til everybody came up there. First Poka and Polie came up. Then Reem came up there, but shit got a little heated when Sexy, Big Grezzy, and Tyrod came up there.

"Happy Birthday nigga! How you like this for a birthday present?" Sexy boast coming in the door with todays newspaper in hand, handing it to me.

Police Blotter

Southern District: April 8 around 12AM a small community experienced a mini massacre, that ended with 3 men dead and 3 more in critical, but stable condition as of now the police don't have any suspects, but they told us their interviewing witnesses.

"Man I seen this shit on the news 7 o'clock this morning at the hotel, I already knew what it was." I say sitting the newspaper down.

"Oh yeah how that turn out?" T-Rod asked.

"Aw man, that bitch tried to turn me out, but that's a whole nother story. Oh yeah I told her we was coming down there tonight, yall wit that shit?"

"Fuck yeah, I gotta go holler at my man Tom-E and get me one of dem skittles," Tyrod says.

"Tyrod you popin pills and blowin money at strip clubs when is you goin give me my stack you owe me" Reem asks.

"I don't owe you no money Reem!"

"So you took that?" Reem says taking a step in Tyrods direction.

"Call it what you want, I said what I had to say about it." T-Rod says with a bland expression on his face.

"Who the fuck you think you talkin to Li.." Reem says throwing a punch before he could finish his sentence. Tyrod jumped back and Reem missed his punch. "Whoa!" "Whole!" We all jump in between them.

"Yo y'all niggaz geeking about a couple of dollars," I said holding them back.

"Nigga lost his mind thinking he goin talk to me like he crazy, Reem says adjusting his shirt collar.

"Whatever Reem I said what I said," Tyrod says. It took about a minute to calm them down enough for them to be in the same room without anybody about to swing on the other.

"Yo what time we goin down the strip club?" Tyrod asked.

"Shorty said she was goin in around 8, so I guess we could go about 9 or 10."

"Well it's 5:30 now," P said.

"Yo let's go out front, it feel good as shit out there im tired of sittin in this mufucka." Glenn says.

"Oh shit, I almost forgot, O and Row said they want us to come down there and see them," Reem told us on our way outside.

"Damn it do feel good out here." I said.

"Ride around Hillside with me Poka, Bean want me to pick him up." P-olie said.

"Yo, why don't we got no guns out this bitch?" I asked.

"My ruger up Robo's, it still got them fucked up bullets in it but it shoot, Glenn says.

"My 380 still in the house, I ain't been in there in damn near 3 days." I say. I'mma pick those guns up from my cousin in the morning, he goin givin me a 21 shot 9mm and a 45 automatic for that tech I gave em. That was his 44 I gave em so it was really like I was just giving it back." Sexy told us.

"Give me a cigarette Grezzy," I said then asked, "Yo what the fuck them cars racin, fuck they drivin like that for?" Only to find out it was the fuzz and they probably was racing, racing to lock our asses up.

"Hands outta your pocket, slowly!" One of the detective's tell me since I was the first he saw.

"All of you up against the wall! Interlock your hands behind your heads." They cuffed everybody who was 18 and over and took us downtown to their homicide interigation building. They didn't put us in a wagon they split us up and threw us in their unmarked cars. We entered the building through the garage and then we were placed in a room together. The room had two sofa's and a automatic metal door that opened and closed electronically. They called us out of the room one at a time or by two's. They called me out of the room with the sofas and brought me into a room with a desk and 3 chairs, two on one side and I sat in the one on the opposite side of the two.

"How you doin Mr. Ray, I'm Detective Malone and this is Detective Gear," the detective said as if I gave a fuck.

"Well since you fella's already know who I am, I don't see the need to introduce myself." I said.

"Of course we know who you are, we know everything that goes on in Cherry Hill." Malone said.

"So what's up, what's all this about?" I asked.

"Just wanna ask you and your boys a couple of questions that alright?" "Shoot, I don't think I can be of much help to you but what the hell," I say then lean back in my chair and fold my arms across my chest.

"Okay well I'm gonna turn on this tape recoder and tape our conversation, is that alright?"

"Whatever," I replied.

(The officer pushed the record button and began to speak.)

"Homicide Detective Dennis Malone along with Detective Raymond Gear proceeding to interview Jamal Ray the date and time is April 8, 2001 time approximately 1800 hours."

"Mr. Ray are you under the influence of any alcohol or other drugs at this time?" They began the questioning.

"No," I lied still rolling from lastnight.

"Are you being forced to make a statement at this current time?"

"No!"

"Do you live in the South Baltimore neighborhood Cherryhill?"

"Yup!"

"How long have you lived in the just mentioned neighborhood?"

"My whole life."

"Where were you on the night of April 7, 2001 from 11:00pm until midnight?"

"I was at a Hotel."

"A Hotel?" One of the detectives repeated with a look of disbelief. "Does this hotel have a name?"

"Ecano's..Econo's." I replied trying to remember the pronunciation of the hotel.

"And were you alone at this hotel Mr. Ray?"

"No!"

"So, who were you with at this hotel?"

"A girl."

"Does she have a name?"

"Yup.. I guess," I replied realizing how stupid its gonna sound that I don't know the girls name.

"Can you tell us this women's name?"

"Don't know it."

"You don't know?" He repeated as he scribbled something in his note-pad "Nope!"

"How long did you stay in the hotel with this women Mr. Ray?"

"All night."

"So let me get this straight, you stayed all night with this woman and you don't know her name?"

"Correct."

"Okay since you wanna play stupid let's switch gears Mr. Ray, where did you go after you were shot at yesterday afternoon?"

(He caught me off guard with that one, I think he knew he would.) "Wha..sho..who m.., naw I don't no wha..ain't nobody shoot me."

(The second detective finally comes alive and starts writing in his little yellow pad.)

"That's not what Glenn told us," Malone says with a smile.

Glenn. yeah right." I say.

"Look man, he's trying to dump the weight on you, now either you can play dumb or you can help yourself out."

"First off, ain't no weight to dump on me, so I don't know what you talking about."

"So you didn't know 3 men were murdered last night?"

"Shit was on the news everybody know."

"So I guess it's just a big coincidence one of those men shoot at you that evening then gets murdered that night?"

"Ain't nobody shoot at me."

"You know that's motive right?"

"I don't know nuffin!"

(This went on for another 5-10 minutes until they took me back to the sofa room where the rest of the guys were.)

"I gotta be to work, can we go?" Reem says when they opened the door to let me in.

"Yeah we been here for damn near 3 hours!" Sexy says to the detective.

"What we goin to do with em Sarge?" One of the detectives asked.

"Fuck it, book all of em." Sarge says.

CHAPTER 20'S INTRO

After Sarge told his detectives to book all of us we zapped out.

"What the fuck you locking us up for?"

"Y'all on some bullshit, what y'all chargin us with?" The only answer we got was "You'll find out when you get your charge papers." So we were taken to central bookings where we were stripped searched, fingerprinted, photoed, then thrown into a group cell after being given a free 10 minute call. Reem, Sexy, Big Greezy, Glenn, Tyrod and I locked up. Ain't this about a bitch!

CHAPTER 20
Ain't this bout a bitch

"Man it stink in this bitch, what the fuck one of y'all niggaz shitted on yourself?" I asked directing my question to the junkies sharing the group cell with us.

"One of these niggaz ill!" (Ill:going through drug withdrawals) Sexy says.

"Slide over unk, Damn, what you trying to boguard the bench?" Glenn says sitting down.

"I can't believe this shit, we suppose to be at the strip club but we in this bitch. What you think they goin to charge us with?" I ask.

"Same shit they questioned us for!" Tyrod says.

"Look, we might be alright cuz I saw this shit on the news this morning, and they said it was only two niggaz. So how the fuck they goin charge six of us?" Reem says.

"How the fuck they know I got shot at?"

"They said something about that?" T-Rod asks.

"Yea, then they told me Glenn told em."

"They said wha..!" Glenn tried to interject but I waved him off letting him know I aint believe that shit then continued telling the story trying to imitate the detectives voice

"Glenns dumping all the weight on you, won't you help yourself out and tell us something."

"Fuck no!" Glenn says.

"I ain't believe em, I told them bitches yeah right."

"That's the type of games them bitches play." Reem said.

"They told me you told em me and Glenn was the shooters you stayed in the car," Tyrod said.

"Yeah they tried to tell me O fallin apart in there, saying Reem killed that nigga." Reem tells us.

"Hell no, they bought up O shit!" Sexy asked.

(After about an hour of trying to figure out what the police where up to we gave up and got comfortable.)

"Naw, fuck that! What's up with Reem tryin to snuff T-Rod, fuck was that about?"

(With time to talk Tyrod ran that day back to Reem and Reem remembered that Tyrod did pay him, long story short Reem apologized and they were back cool.)

"Scotty you ain't never tell us what had happened with you and the stripper bitch," Glenn said.

"What you wanna know about?" I asked then began to brag a little, "How we sipped champagne in the shower, or how I got some head in the hot-tub? I mean what's up, what you wanna know?"

"I wanna know why you said she tried to turn you out?" Sexy says.

"You would ask about that shit, man that bitch a freak, I wasn't wit none of that shit she was talkin about."

"What yo?" Tyrod asked.

"The bitch tried to sneak one in on me." I said trying to dodge answering the question infull.

"What yo?"

"What she try do?" They all asked demanding answers.

"Look don't nobody laugh!" I said.

"Ain't nobody goin laugh, what happened?"

"The bitch licked my gouch."

"What the fuck is your gouch, your asshole?"

"Naw, I just found out what it is last night, it's the space between your butt and your nuts."

"Ah! ha! ha! ha!, it's the what?"

"I told you niggaz not to laugh."

"Aight you just caught a nigga off guard with that gouch shit."

"What it is again?" Sexy baited me into repeating myself jus for their amusement.

"It's the space between ya butt and ya nuts."

"Yo how the fuck she get her face right there, you let that bitch lick ya ass an ain't trying tell us?"

"Yo, she did not lick my ass, she tried I told you I told her I wasn't wit that shit."

"Well how she get pass your ass to get to ya gouch?"

"She came from the front way, look it was like this! She was sitting on the end of the bed, and I was standing in front of her getting the head, that's when I threw one leg up on the bed, and was fucking her face, that's when she laid on the bed, but my leg ended up like on her shoulder more, less then she started goin to work on my balls and before I know it she slid her tongue across my gouch. The shit caught me off guard, I thought she made a mistake and did it at first but she kept doin that shit. Then the bitch tried to turn me on my stomach that's when I had to stop the bitch."

"Ah, ha ha ha hell no!" Everybody got a laugh at my expense but fuck what they talkin bout im thinking bout that bitch right now.

We sat in the group cell and tripped off of each other for hours until we noticed everybody was getting charge papers and going to see the commissioner but us.

"Yo it's mornin out that bitch, we been in this cell for at least 10 hours and ain't got no charge papers yet, that's crazy!" Greezy said. "Ayy! Ay! C.O. where we at on that list to see the commissioner?" Sexy yells to the correctional officer through the crack in the door.

"Fuck that," Reem whispers then in the same breathe yells, "Where the fuck is our charge papers!"

"We can't see the commissioner without no charge papers." Glenn says.

An hour later breakfast came, a six ounce styrafoam cup of dry cereal, a 1/2 pint of milk, four slices of bread, two boiled eggs, two packs of jelly, Oh and a four ounce orange juice.

"I'm not eatin this shit," I say looking into my brown breakfast bag. "Let me get it nephew." The last Unc left said to me.

"Don't none of y'all want this shit?" I asked my niggaz.

"Naw," they all replied.

"Give me your juice Unk you could have the whole bag."

"Shit, give it here nephew."

Damn near 3 hours after breakfast and still nothin everybody left the group cell but us and niggaz was starting to get frustrated.

"Boom! Boom! Boom! Boom! Boom! Boom!" Sexy kicked the metal door until an officer opened it.

"What the hell's your problem man?" The officer asked.

"We've been here since yesterday and ain't seen no commissioner, ain't got no charge papers!" Sexy told the C.O.

"Alright calm down, what's your name's?" The C.O. asked.

We all gave him our names and a half hour later..

Davon Shields, Kareem Glover, Glenn Chase, Jamal Ray, Tyrod Roads, Kurtis Williams come with me." The officer tells us.

"Where we goin, we ain't even get no charge papers!" We protested.

"Just stay to the left of the hallway and keep walking."

An hour later we were all free, released without charges.

(Note to you pussy niggaz, see what can happen if everybody keep their mouth closed.)

CHAPTER 21'S INTRO

When I got in the house fatigue set in on me, I had been woke for the last 3 days but I still managed to shower before I crashed. My grandmother tried to scold me about not seeing me since 8 o'clock AM Thursday and here it is 1pm on Saturday and I'm getting out of hand and blah, blah, blah I wanted to rationalize with her but I needed some sleep. I slept all of Saturday and woke up at about 10 o'clock the next morning and my grandmother was still one my case and she had my grandfather backing her up so I didn't stand a chance. My grandfather normally stays out of shit but I didn't know what gotten in to him,

cuz he's letting me have it too.

CHAPTER 21
Trouble at home

"You either goin to work or you gonna go to school and that's all to it. I'm 60 years old and I get up every morning and go to work, so I be damned if imma have you laying around here doing nothing." My grandfather said.

"Your 18 now Jamal so we can only do and say so much, it's going to come down to what choice you wanna make for yourself." My granny added.

"I go to school, I just be getting there late sometimes and they don't mark me on roll." I said in my defense.

"Well son, if your not on roll your not there that's like me goin to work and not clocking in, does that make any sense to you?" My grandfather asked.

"No, but that's different, you.."

Beep! Beep! Beep! Beep!

I checked my pager and it was Reem, so I went upstairs to use the phone and get away from my interrogators.

"What up Reem?" I say through the phone.

"Yo I'm about to go see O, ride with me so you can visit Row we goin to pull em together."

"I'm in the house, just blow the horn'."

"Aight!"

"Aight," I said then hung up the phone.

About a half hour later Reem beep'd his horn and I was on my way out the door but not without a warning from my grandfather first.

"You remember what I said son, either you goin work or you goin go ta school. If you can't do that you goin have to find you some place to live." With that comment we locked eyes neither one of us breaking our stare until..Honk! Honk! Honk! I just smiled and continued out the door.

"My grandfather a sucker!" I say as I sit down in the passenger seat of Reems Buick.

"What he do shorty?" Reem asked.

"Talking about putting a nigga out and shit," I say lighting a cigarette. "Crack that window, what he heard you runnin around out here shootin niggaz?" Reem asked.

"Naw, I don't think so anyway he on some crazy shit talkin bout either imma go to school or imma have to get a job or get out."

"What's crazy about that?"

"It's just how he said it, Or you can find somewhere else to live." Me and Reem rode down the jail talking about the police and if he thought they had anything on us. He said probably not, they were just shaken our bush to see if any leave's drop. When we got to the jail which happened to be right next door to the central booking facility we just spend our Friday night in. It was only a few people in line in front of us, we got in and had to place all of our belongings in a locker then walk thru a metal detector before we we're escorted upstairs to the horseshoe style visiting area. With the prisoners sittin inside the horseshoe styled table and their visitor's on the opposite side. We were allowed to slap hands or hug our visitors at the beginning and end of our visit.

"What's up? Reem said y'all wanted us to come see y'all. Y'all ain't know we was ready to be over this bitch wit y'all?" I say to O and Row who are seated across from me and Reem.

"Yeah you know we hear everything first over the jail, the streets talk and they say y'all runnin wild out that bitch." O says.

"Y'all got T.V's over here, yall ain't see she that shit on the news a couple days ago?"

"Yeah we was watching that shit in the dayroom, one of the niggaz that got killed was the nigga I showed you at the party Scotty you remember him?"

"Yeah I remember that bitch, Row what the fuck you get your haircut for? You ugly ass shit."

"I had to get my shit cut, I had to get 6 stitches in my head bitch ass nigga stabbed me in my head twice and in my back a couple of times."

"Fuck no, who, for what?"

"Suppose to be the nigga ONE EYE cousin."

"Where he from, out our way?"

"I ain't never seen the nigga out there." Row tells me.

"You aight though, what the fuck he stab you wit?"

"A knife, what you think?"

"Look listen up yall," O said and the four of us huddled in a little closer as O talked in a whisper.

"Look I got my motions back and.."

"What the fuck are motions?" I immataurely interrupted.

"It's all the evidence the state has in your case and everybody who made a statement that kinda shit but look I found out who the witnesses is in our case, I got their address and everything. I might need y'all to pay a couple people a visit."

"Anything for you O," I said.

"Aight good, just wait imma let yall know what or who to do first." "Look Bro, I wanted to ask you if it was anyway you could set something up with the Florida connect for me cuz I've been hollering at the old connect and it seem like his coke getting worser and worser."

Yeah, I'll see if I can set something up, how the block doing though?" "Man it's aight, but it ain't how it was before you left." I said I was about to say something else about the block until Reem kick'd me in the leg.

"What the fuc.."

"Mouse just ran across my foot you seen that shit Scotty?"

"Naw, I felt it though," I say looking at Reem like he crazy for kicking me. I felt good after seeing O and Row, I mean it was fucked up they were locked up but I ain't seen them niggaz in a couple months and it was kinda refreshing talking to them.

(On the ride home.)

"You stupid as shit Scotty!" Reem said then asked, "Why you say that? I'm trying to get O to set me up with the outta town connect and you was about to tell him how fucked up the block is."

"Hell yeah I was geekin wasn't I?"

"Yeah you was geekin, you know how protective he is about shit like that."

"Yo why ain't nobody else come down here wit us to see them niggaz?"

"P-olie took Bean and Poka to a car auction and I guess everybody else was sleep or laid up or something cuz ain't nobody answer my page."

"Why Dem niggaz ain't tell nobody they was goin to the auction?"

"You the one that ain't come outside yesterday, niggaz was talkin bout that shit up Robo's."

When we got back to the hood Reem stopped me past my house so I could grab my gun then he dropped me off down Angie's house.

So as I'm walking from the parking lot to Angies house I hear, "A you, hold up a minute." It was two uniform cops along with one of those homicide detectives.

"Hold up for what?" I asked still walking.

"We need to ask you a few questions the uniform says."

"Sorry, im in a hurry, I don't have time to answer any questions right now."

"Ay, you look familiar, do I know you?" The homicide detective ask. Now at this time im still a good 15 to 20 yards ahead of them, so I could take off running and most likely get away but I ain't on the block hustling they ain't see me doing shit so what I gotta run for and I'm in front of my girls door. "Naw, I don't think you know me we probably all just look alike out here, Ay Angie!" I yell up at the window.

"What's your name man?" The homicide detective ask now he's only about 15 feet away.

"I don't have to talk to y'all, im mindin my business and yall wanna fuck wit somebody."

"Do you have ID on you sir?" One of the uniforms say reaching out at my arm.

"You ain't gotta touch me!" I say swatting his hand away. The second uniform puts his hand on his gun as if he's about to draw it.

"Place your hands on the wall for me sir!" The first uniform tells me. Shit, I should of ran when I had the fuckin chance. now I'm thinkin should I push officer 1 into officer 2 and make a break for it. If I don't get away I can at least get the gun off of me.

"Sir I'm not gonna ask you again, hands on the wall now!" Nah, I think imma go with the push and run I think to myself.

"Is there a problem officers?" Ms. Vanessa says standing in the doorway. "No, just go back in the house ma'am."

"Fine as long as my son is going in with me."

"This is your son ma'am?"

"Yes, now is there a problem, did he do something wrong?"

"No we just wanted to ask him a few questions, that's all."

"I just told yall I don't wanna talk to yall!" I say aggresively stepping up on Angie's porch.

"Well does he have to talk to yall?" Ms. Vanessa asks.

"No.. well it's just with the recent murders were pretty much trying to talk to anyone who frequents this area."

"Well, sorry sir, but my son doesn't know anything about that."

"Alright, well thank you ma'am."

"Scotty, what the hell is goin on with you?" Miss Vanessa asked once we got in the house.

"What do yo mean?"

"I just got out of the car and they told me to come here."

"That's not what I'm talking about."

"Well what you talkin about?"

"Did you kill those boys?"

"No!"

"Well I had to ask, why didn't you come back down here or at least call?" "I know I'm sorry, that was inconsiderate but I didn't find out about the shooting until the next morning."

"Aw it was awful, I didn't think they would ever stop shooting and were those boys shooting at you when we got back from dinner?"

"It was all just a big misunderstanding Miss Vanessa nothing you need to worry about."

"Says you, but I gotta get to work so I will talk to you later, Angie's in the shower. Tell her I said to call me if she wants me to bring home dinner."

"Aight Miss V"

"Alright Scotty!" She says with a cynical smirk.

CHAPTER 22'S INTRO

As time went by it seems like shit was just getting worst and worst, I don't even know where to start at. They lock Lil Greezy up for an attempt murder on Pelle Pelle because he got caught with the gun that Bean shot Pelle Pelle with. (The first time he got shot.) Now I don't know why or how they plan on going about prosecuting that case since Pelle Pelle is now dead. I fell asleep down Angie's house and my beeper kept going off and she called the number back while I was sleep and my stripper not only told Angie about us, but she rubbed it in her face. So I woke up to fist an tears, this was over a month ago and I'm still trying to make amends for that. I guess you could call it a declaration of my love or whatever you wanna call it but some dude at school was pressin up on Angie. I don't know if she was inviting the shit, because of the incident with the stripper, but I stabbed the dude a couple of times. He told on me initially but Keyco hollered at him and he supposed to not be pressing charges but the warrant was already issued so I ain't been to school since. The block hot, Reem trying to charge niggaz 1100 for a ounce and 12 hunnit if he gotta front it to you. Just a little over a month ago I was almost up to $10,000 in my dresser. Last time I counted my money I had $1,800. Ecstacy is a hell of a drug, I have been partying like everyday is my birthday fucking wit Glenn. Sexy and greezy they party too but me and Glenn party all night. Sexy found him a girl, some teacher bitch, she cool..cool as shit for real. Sexy had her bring me a gun one time under strange circumstances she might of saved my life for real, but that's another story. Poka and P-olie set up a strip behind Ki-Ki's house they doin aight. Bean, every since he brought that Thunderbird from the auction he can't sit still long enough to hustle. I guess that sum's up everybody. Oh shit, T-Rod, can't forget my nigga T-Rod, ain't shit really change wit him he met some new bitch he told me she rich or something but I ain't met her yet. Aight so where does that leave us. Oh, O and Row they start trial today I ain't been back down the jail to see them since I have a warrant. Reem said O said his lawyer says he's going to get the case thrown out. They won't even make it to trial, let's see.

CHAPTER 22

The Trial

August 1, 2001

-Clarence Mitchell Courthouse-

The state calls case number Blah, Blah, Blah, Blah, Blah, Blah, Blah, Blah, Otis Glover and Roland Henson vs The State of Maryland.

The defendants are charged with the murder of Sam "ONE EYE" Tyson.

At the arraignment both defendants entered a plea of not guilty. The state offered a plea deal of 50 years all suspended but 20 years.

"As I understand it, no agreement could be made on a plea so are both sides ready for trial?" The judge asked.

"Your honor, Walter Brown representing client Otis Glover and Margrette Read representing client Roland Henson. We the defense ask that this case is dismissed due to a Tainted Photo Array and cohersion of the states lead witness."

It took the judge all of 10 seconds to say "Motion to dismiss denied. trial set for 1 o'clock."

So we recessed to 1 o'clock when we got back to the courtroom they had jury selection and a motion hearing. Where all 10 of the defense's motion's were denied and the state was scheduled to call it's first witness at 9AM the next morning.

August 2, 2001 9:15AM

-Clarence Mitchell Courthouse-.

"The state call it's first witness Officer Gary Worthy," the states attorney begins her prosecution.

"Officer Worthy on the night of Feb 15th of this present year, you were the first officer to report to the scene of a shooting in the Cherryhill community can you tell us what you observed when you arrived on the scene?" "Well when I got on the scene, I noticed the victim Sam Tyson laying on his back in a puddle of his own blood with injury wounds to his chest, neck, and face." Officer Worthy said then looked up at the defendants as if he knew they were responsible. The states attorney began with her next question.

"And at that time did you have any suspects in the case?"

"Yes!"

"And who were the suspects at that time?"

"Well a few hours before Mr. Tyson was murdered our C.I. inform.." "Excuse me Officer Worthy" the states attorney cut in, but can you please explain C.I. to the court."

"C.I, Confidential Informant."

"Okay, carry on".

"My CI informed me that One Eye".

"One Eye?"

"Excuse me, Sam One Eye Tyson was responsible for the kidnapping of Roland Henson, and a few hours before the murder of Mr. Tyson there was an attempt made on Mr. Tyson's life but he escaped with a minor injury to the leg. The leg injury was confirmed by our medical examiner". "Object!"

"There's no proof of any alleged kidnapping and if Mr. Tyson was or was not shot previous to his murder my client was never questioned, detained, or convicted so it has no relevance to this case your honor." Row's lawyer interjected.

"The state's just establishing motive your honor."

"Stick to the facts pertaining to this case counselor, objection overruled."

"So your informant Mr. Worthy lead you in the direction of?"

"The Wallboys, a drug organization that frequents the 2600 block of Spelman Rd.

"And who exactly are The Wallboys Mr. Worthy?"

"Well Otis here is the head of and supplier of the gang and.."

"Object! Propaganda!"

"Sustain counsel."

The state lead the witness/police office for about another 8 minutes of testimony which really should have been two minutes, but the defense had to object to every question damn near until the state's attorney must of got tired of it and told O and Row's lawyers "your witness counselors."

"Mr. Worthy, I'd like to first address your statement of your "Confidential Informant" O's lawyer started, "now you make this C.I. sound like he's a member of a special police unit but from my experience as an attorney all quote, unquote confidential informants are nothing more than coke heads you use t.."

"Object!" The state's attorney said.

"Your honor the officer has painted an unclear picture of his C.I. and since we can't bring forth this C.I. so the jury can judge his or her credibility for themselves I just wanted to make sure they understood what a C.I. actually was," Walter Brown said.

"Objection overruled, you may proceed."

"As I was saying C.I.'s are nothing more than coke user's who in exchange for their cooperation with officers are overlooked for there pettie drug possession," O's lawyer poked holes in the prosecutions theory, then to have Row's lawyer finish him off.

"Mr. Worthy, so after you were informed that Mr.Tyson was shot and had a man held against his will, what was it that you did with that information?"

"Since I had no proof I.."

Row's lawyer haulted the officer before he could say another word.

"Thank You Officer Worthy, the defense is done with this witness," Row's lawyer said letting his last words rest with the jury.

"Since I had no proof."

Walter Brown and Margette Read exchanged words in each other's ear when the judge said.

"Miss Read your witness."

"I have no questions for Mr. Worthy your honor," she replied.

"The state would like to call it's next witness, Sargent Jeffrey Folks"

"Sargent Folks as I understand it, a positive identification was made of the two defendants to you?" The states attorney begun with her second witness.

"Yes ma'am!" The sergent responded.

"And can you explain to the court how the positive ID was made?"

"Well it was about 10 days after the murder of Mr. Tyson and we were starting to get a little discouraged because the more time that passes the harder these cases become to solve, usually! It is about 10 days after the murder and im in the station going over some paperwork and in comes Mr. Marshall."

"Mr. Marshall?" The states attorney repeated.

"Yes Mr. Vincent Marshall came to my desk and said he had information about the murder that happened a little while ago. So after he ran his story down to me I went and got the tape recorder. He made a recorded statement and we issued warrants for the two defendants we identified."

"And Sargent Folks did Mr. Marshall say why it took him so long to come forth with the information he gave you?" The state's attorney asked.

"Yes, he said he feared for his life because he knew first hand what the Wallboys were capable of doing."

"And the two people that he identified, do you see them in the courtroom?"

"Yes, the two defendants seated behind the defense table."

"Thank you, no further questions."

Row's lawyer stood up to cross examine the Sargent.

"Sargent Folks you say you were at your desk when Mr. Marshall approached you with information about the murder?"

"Yes, that is correct".

"I am going to now ask you to do me and the rest of the courtroom a favor, could you draw a mental picture for us where your desk is located inside the precinct."

"I'd say the northwest corner of the station."

"Let me try again Sargent Folks, matter of fact let me just start you off. I walk thru the main entrance and then.."

"Okay, well you walk thru the main entrance thru the mental detector and you enter the lobby/breakroom, walk down the west hall and my office is the next to last door on your right."

"You say west hallway, is there another hallway besides the west?" Mrs. Read asked.

"Well yes, there's the east hall".

"And around what time is it when Mr. Marshall came to you with the information?"

"About 6:30, 7 o'clock maybe."

"PM?"

"Yes PM!"

"And on average how many officers are in the precinct at this time?"

"Could be anywhere from 6 to 12."

"So let me get this straight, Mr. Marshall walks in from off the street and navigates himself past over a half dozen officers and TA'DAH appears at your desk with this magical information about the murder."

"Yeah, something like that."

"Is this the normal way civilians present information to your district, do you normally let civilians roam freely through your precinct?"

"Well, no but.."

"Well how is it that civilian Vincent Marshall just happened to achieve this?" Mrs. Read demanded.

"Maybe one of my.."

"No Sargent Folks! Maybe is not sufficient when you have two men's live's hanging in the balance. I interviewed Vincent Marshall and he told me a completely different story, now maybe I should remind you of the penalty of perjury before I ask you again! Now how did Vincent Marshall get to your precinct and then your office?"

"Like I said before, I was in my office when Vincent Marshall rounded the corner of my open door and walked in. I never said who brought him

or how he got there, I just told you what happened when he got there."
"Alright that will be all officer Folks."

"Well were going to recess for lunch until 1 o'clock, I expect every one back here who needs to be back here and the state ready to call their next witness." The judge instructed.

1:23pm

"The state calls its next witness Mr. Vincent Marshall," the states attorney began after recess.

"Mr. Marshall I hold here a copy of the statement you made on February 24th, 2001. Is that your signature there at the bottom?" The state's attorney asked Vincent walking up to the witness stand giving him a closer look at the paperwork in her hand.

"Yes, yes it is."

"And do you remember making this statement?"

The state's attorney begins to read from the paper.

"..as I was leaving the block. I saw a black or dark blue sedan pull up with three men occupying the vehicle. I had to look twice because the driver of the vehicle had a mask over his face and as I turned to look at the the other men occupying the vehicle they pulled their mask over their face also. I began to walk faster trying to hurry off of the block, I never looked back but about 10 seconds later I heard shots ring out behind me. that's when I broke off into a jog or slow run." The S.A finished reading then looked up and asked, "do you remember making this statement Mr. Marshall?"

"Yes!"

"Were you forced or threatend by anyone to make this statement?"
"No!"

"And do you see the men you identified in the photo array?"
"Yes!"

"Could you please point them out to the jury?" The S.A said barely able to hide her excitement of almost securing her first murder convictions.

"Yes, the two gentlemen sitting at the defense table."

"Thank you Mr. Marshall I have no further questions."

Margrette Read stood up to begin her cross examination.

"Mr. Marshall on May 6, I had my private investigator interview you about the events that took place on February 10th and 24ᵗʰ of 2001 correct."

"Yes, I believe so."

"And on what date you told my investigator, correct me if I'm wrong will you Mr. Marshall, you told my investigator that you where caught by Baltimore Police Officer with 3 capsules of heroin and 2 vails of cocaine. Afterwards you were taken to Southern District Police station to a holding cell. When you were approached by detective Wako and asked if you knew anything about any of the recent shootings in the area. That's when you made a statement similar to the one read by the state's attorney. But in your statements you didn't mention seeing anyone's face, all you saw was a car pull up with 3 men in it wearing mask and shortly after you heard gun shots. That's when the detective asked you if you wanted to help yourself out and offered in exchange for your signature in a photo array he would make the drugs you where caught with disappear. Is this statement correct Mr. Marshall?"

"I'd like to plead the 5th," Marshall responded and the courtroom immediately broke into chaos.

CHAPTER 23'S INTRO

After the dramatic closing arguments from O and Rows lawyers the jury came back with a verdict of Not Guilty. After being released they both chilled out with their family for a couple of days. My father told me that the police came by granny's house looking for me and said they would be back, so I took the fiend Ms. Rose up on her offer on the room for rent. After about the second week of staying with her we grew a bond and she wouldn't charge me by the night or week she would just ask me for a couple dollars here and there or I would give her a couple of pills or whatever. She started to look at me like her son, I guess she was surprised at how respectful and shit I was. Jennifer lived right across the street from Ms. Rose so Glenn would stay with her to be closer to me. Me and Glenn got real tight around this time, you rarely ever saw him without me or me without him and we both was fully loaded. I still had my 380, he broke into somebody's house looking for money and drugs all he found was a Beretta 9 and a couple of hundred dollars. It was a good thing O was home because I was all the way fucked up, almost. I took my last thousand dollars and brought a pound of weed because I smoked so much when I had the E pills in me it seemed like a smart idea to be able to smoke for free. Glenn brought a half of pound with the couple of hundred dollars he got off of his B&E, so that's what it was. It's mid August and it's a nice day out and im still feeling my E pills from last night, so I grabbed my orange juice out the fridge and went on the front porch to smoke my blunt. I got on hooping shorts and a tank top so I throw my 380 under the cushion on the front porch chair and then sat in the chair next to that one, that's when O pulled up.

CHAPTER 23
Home Sweet Home

"What's up shorty?" O says getting out of his Acura.

"You what's up my nigga," I say as we slap hands then embrace in a man hug.

"Reem was telling me shit crazy out chere, he says y'all niggaz poppin E's and you wife'n a fiend. Shorty I ain't been gone that long." O says with his signature laugh following his words.

"Cut the shit nigga, ain't nobody tell you im wife'n no fiend!" I say defensively.

"Naw, I'm just fuckin wit you, you out here in ya pajamas and shit. I don't know though, I know you ain't out here slippin in slippers." O says realizing that someone might want to retaliate for the murder he just beat.

"I might got on slippers but I ain't slippin," I say lifting the cushion so O can see the gun.

"Okay, Okay I see ain't that much changed." O says.

"Man what's up, you ready to put this shit back together?" I asked blowing out smoke from my blunt.

"I don't know man, I have been scoping shit out these last couple of days and I been getting a bad vibe. I mean, I ain't gonna sit around and do nothing. I just don't know what imma do yet."

"Come in for a minute," I say to O grabbing my gun from under the cushion and opening the door. We go upstairs, I unlocked my room door with the small key that fit the door knob and me and O walk in the room.

I grab the weed which was a couple ounces over a half of pound out of my bottom drawer.

"The nigga Whoodie sold me a pound of this for 900, he wanted a stack but.. you know."

"Do this shit sell? I mean I know it sell but.. how much you make a day?"

"I ain't even goin to lie, I be bullshittin. I move around so much with weed you need a place where people can depend on you being at but I still make a couple of hunnit of dollars a day and that's not even with trying. I'm just saying its something to think about."

"Yeah, I will think about it." O says then changes the subject which isn't a good sign that he will invest in the weed.

"This house clean as shit, even your room clean. I thought you'd be livin like a lil viking," O says tapping me trying to get me to laugh at his joke. I jus smirk and say, "Yeah I know right but naw Rose clean up for me every other day, I ain't gotta do shit for real just look out for her."

"What kinda profit you make off of the whole pound?" "O" asked sniffing a ounce out the bag.

"Well the whole pound was 16 ounces I could sell them whole a hunnit, a hunnit twenty five a ounce, maybe. Or if I bag up the whole pound I will bag up about $3,000, that's a aight lil flip if it move fast."

"So what, you wanna turn The Wall into a weed strip?" O asked me earnestly.

"Man The Wall is hot!" I responded sounding counter-productive to my proposal.

"Is the Wall hot or is y'all hot, cause if its y'all the heat goin follow wherever we set up shop at."

"Its probably a lil bit of both, police been acting like some real dick heads lately."

"Yeah, they get like that once bodies and shit start dropping. Yo I met this nigga in the joint, a nigga from over West Baltimore. He was getting a whole bunch of dope money at one point in time, long story short the nigga put me on some legal shit. He fuckin with the dump trucks, tractor trailers, and shit. That's good money just for driving then if we hustling and driving we save up enough money to buy our own trucks that's when the real money comes into play."

"Dump trucks? I ain't even got my permit let alone a license to drive a dump truck."

"Only thing that's stoping you is you, I see Bean and em riding around with no license. Don't be like them and fuck your driving record up. You got any tickets?"

"Naw," I respond while tossing the dumptruck idea around in my head.

"Scotty! Glenn at the door, Rose yelled up the steps breaking my concentration.

"Let em in!" I yelled back.

"Shorty CDL's ain't hard to get, we can study the book together while you getting your permit and shit." O says.

"Fuck it, I trust you so it's whatever O."

"What that nigga O'fficial up here, I see the TL out front!" Glenn says walking in the room.

"What up Glenn!"

"What up O," they exchange greetings then Glenn goes on to say,

"Scotty why the fuck you ain't answer the phone last night?"

"I was high as shit on the phone with Angie, yo I don't be clicking over I ain't wit all that."

"I had a bitch for you, Jennifer home girl Rell was over there last night. We was over there playin spades all night for real." Glenn informs me.

"Man Scotty was in here fuckin Rose Glenn, you can believe he was on the phone if you want!"

"I knew you was fuckin her." Glenn says consigning with O.

"Fuck both of y'all, ain't nobody fuckin that lady."

"Scotty, I wanted you to go over Vick house wit me, I got this half of brick my lil cousins want me to cook for him. I'mma bring back a extra 6 ounces off it, you think you could help me get rid of em?"

"What you about ta do Glenn?" I asked.

"I'm bout go pick my money up from my lil man down Bethune and give him some more bags then im goin home and take a shower, oh I gotta go see my son too. Walk around Chardae house when you finish with O." Glenn says.

(Soon as I finished up with O I went to my new lay spot and put up the 6 ounces up. Soon as I came out the door Big Greezy was pulling up with Sexy in the car so the three of us rode around Chardae's house.)

"Glenn's upstairs in my room, y'all can go up there." Chardae says as she lets us in.

"What's up y'all?" I say, speaking to Chardae and her homegirls that where sitting in the living room.

"Don't fuckin speak to me," Marie replies.

"Well what's up everybody except Marie!"

"Fuck you Scotty!"

"Why are you beefing wit me? You geekin shorty!"

"I ain't geekin, you phony and you know you phony."

"Whatever yo," I say to Marie and proceed towards the stairs.

"Ya lil man jamming down that bitch, that's all you got left?" I say to Glenn as he's sitting on the bed bagging up his last couple of ounces, with a lit blunt hangging out his mouth.

"Ell me a oughta," Glenn says with the blunt still hanging.

"Let me help you out," I say grabbing the blunt from between his lips. "Now lets try that one more time, take it from the top."

"I said sell me a quarter Scotty, you act like you don't understand English."

"Sell you a quarter of what, that coke I just got?" I asked

"Naw, sell me a quarter pound out of that grass you got left."

"Why you ain't call Whoodie?"

"He said he waiting for his man to come back from New York that could be a couple of days."

"Give me 450!"

"450, that's crazy Scotty! How you goin to tax me?"

"I know what you gettin it for."

"I ain't taxin you nigga that's a good price, matter fact give me 400." I say feeling like $450 was a little steep.

"I was goin ask you let me get it for 250."

"250! You trippin, Homeboys, this book I'm reading told me about this give me 350 and that's my final offer!" I say thinking about how Law #2 jus told me how friends become spoiled.

We sat around Chardae house and smoked about 8 dutch's Grezzy and Sexy passed out. Them niggaz drinkers they ain't no smokers. I helped Glenn bag up his last couple of bags, then he picked Greezy's pocket for his car keys and we drove on Bethune to take Glenn's lil man the bags we bagged up. Of course we could of went straight back around Chardae's after dropping off the weed but we was too fly and too high and it felt too good outside soo...

"Yo, drive down T-rod's and see if Del and em back on wit the pills yet." I instructed Glenn.

"It was live as shit down by Tyrod house the girls on the corner house was having a cookout, they had stand-up basketball goals out in the street it was niggaz and bitch's everywhere. Del front porch was live Poka and P-olie was down there..ain't nuffin like summertime in the hood.

"I know I could sell a couple of bags down here," I say to glenn as we're getting out of the car.

"I gave my lil man all the bags I had," Glenn says.

"Oh, what you think you goin smoke all my bags up today, huh?"

"You need to cut it out, you ain't never act like this Scotty."

"Like what?"

"Petty!"

"Ain't nobody Petty, im broke nigga."

"O back you be aight, you know ya father goin make sure you straight."
"I ain't never been son'd out."

"Ay Scotty!" P-olie yells and signals me to come here.

"What up, P?"

"Man, I was just ready to come looking for you, when the fuck you goin get another beeper. Ya stupid ass goin throw ya shit against a wall, cause you got jammed up with ya stripper bitch."

"Fuck that beeper, what's up?"

"O told me.. well I brought 2 and a quarter from O, he told me to get it from you."

"When you want it?" We got the car, "I can go grab it for you right now if you want."

"Yeah grab that shit, me and Poka ain't got nothing left for real." "Glenn ride me up my house..Rose house right quick, I can grab that weed for you too while we up there!" I said trying to entice Glenn to put a move on it.

After grabbing the coke for P and the weed for Glenn we head back to the car only to be stopped short by Jennifer and her home girl Rell. "Here he go right here Rell, you was on my heels last night for him so don't try front on my man now." Glenn said.

"Glenn you a clown yo, why you trying put me on blast?" Rell said with a smile then asked me.

"So why didn't you answer the phone last night, you ain't feel like being bothered?"

"Naw, it wasn't that, I umm, I wasn't expecting no calls and sometimes Rose be turning the ringer off."

"Oh, so what y'all about ta do?"

"Ride back down the hill, where y'all on y'all way to?"

"Up the store, drop us off." Jennifer asked.

"Come on."

In the car me and Rell exchanged numbers and a little small talk, then me & Glenn stopped back at Chardae's and picked up Greezy and Sexy. Greezy threatened to fuck us up and all that other shit but we knew he wasn't goin to do shit. We're like family the whole wall, all of us so we knew he would get over it. He's shooting off at the mouth as we're making our way to the door.

"Y'all think cuz y'all caught a couple lil bodies, attempts or whatever a nigga won't put his foot in y'all ass, y'all just start doin this shit. I've been shootin niggaz since 96 so that shit don't impress me."

"Yo I gotta go to the bathroom I'll meet y'all in the car," I say to get away from Grezzy he was blowing my high.

When I came out the bathroom I almost ran into Chardae.

"Damn what you goin knock me over?" Chardae said as I weave her.

"I ain't even see ya black ass, better cut a light on around this mu-fucka!" I say jokingly to Charade.

"Ha, funny hold on right fast Scotty." Chardae said.

"What's up yo?"

"Yo why..never mind."

"Don't do me like that Chardae, I hate when people do that shit tell me yo," I say thinking she was about to tell me something Rell said.

"Yo why..why that nigga Greezy grabbed my ass, then tried to put his tongue in my mouth."

"He did what? Fuck no!" I said in disbelief.

"Yo, I put that shit on my son, that nigga wild. I know me and Glenn ain't officially together but still."

(Honk! Honk! Hooonk!)

"Yo im..imma.. yo I don't know what imma do just let me think for a minute that just fucked me up right there. I'll be back to holler at yall."

"Damn what you was in there taking a shit?" Greezy said when I got back in the car.

"What's wrong Scotty, why you looking like that..you aight?" Glenn asked. Snapping me out of my lil daze. "Yeah, yeah I'm good, Marie lil ass crazy I say playing if off".

CHAPTER 24'S INTRO

We rode back down T-Rod's block with Grezzy still crying about us taking his keys. When we got down there and put our pills in us he finally shut up, at least about his car anyway, which was good because it took everything in me not to let him have it about Chardae. We party'd & bullshitted down the hill all day for real. Me and Glenn caught a ride to the bar then had the ride drop us off over Chardae's house around 11:30 that night, only to find Chardae strangely home alone. I stayed over there for an hour or so sipping and smoking with Chardae and Glenn hopin one of her homegirls came over there but they didn't so I left sometime after midnight. It was only about a 10 to 15 minute walk from Chardae's house to Rose's, it felt good outside I was strapped and high, hoping I would run across a stragler. I ain't see nothing but fiends the whole walk home "shorty you got something?" I had to turn dowm about 8 sales in the 10 minutes it took me to get to the house. That reminded me I need to bag some of that coke up before O sell it all by the ounce on me. Fuck that I need to make me a couple of dollars off that shit so im on my way in the house when I see a couple of chicks on Jennifer's porch so I walked over there. They were on the porch with about a half of 5th of Hennessy left. It was a couple of em over there by them I mean Slater Girls. It was Jennifer, Jessica, Kelly, Rell, and Rell's older sister Nae who happens to be Jennifer's neighbor. So I drank a lil cup of their Hennessy, they talked me out of a bag of weed and talked me into rolling it for them. After that I told em let me take my ass in the house for y'all talk me out of my clothes. Yeah it was a lame shot at humor, but it beats a blank. Anyway Rell asked if I wanted any company, she said she would walk over there once she was finished with her homegirls.

CHAPTER 24
- Rell-

"Boy I don't want no damn pineapples on the pizza," Rell said shaking her head at me.

"Ay, Ay just put pineapples on half of the pizza, yeah. I still want everything else on the rest of the pizza." I said thru the phone.

"Aight just call back when you get out front."

"Pineapples, boy you're disgusting!"

"Don't knock it to you try it!"

"I'll pass."

"Yo I'm ready to get in the shower, if the pizza man comes pay for it." I say emptying my pockets putting my money and shit on the dresser.

"How much is it?"

"12 something just give him 15 dollars, let him keep the change." I took about a 20 minute shower then came back in the room in some gray gap sweat pants and a white tank top. Rell was sitting on the edge of the bed playing Need 4 Speed on the Playstation.

"Pizza man ain't call?" I say drying my hair.

"Naw, some girl called, I told her you told her you were in the shower." "Fuck no, no you didn't, did she ask.."

"Boy calm down, im just joking! You look like you was ready to have a heart attack!"

"Naw, it's just..it's a long story." I say grabbing my deodorant out of the closet.

"Secret, you wear Secret deodorant, I see your a real mans man."

"Ha Ha the jokes just don't stop with you I see, anyway it's fresh scent not none of that girlie shit and I don't have to explain myself."

"Ay, your secrets safe with me!" She says still joking.

"And, your not coming in first place," I say playfully slapping the Playstation controller out of her hand watching the blue Lamborghini speed past her. I thought it was going to be a shitty night after Rell told me she was on her period but it wasn't we played playstation, ate pizza, smoked a blunt together then fell asleep watching The Bone Collector. The next morning I was halfway done bagging up an ounce when Rell woke up.

"Um, what time is it?" She asked while yawning. "

Two of."

"Two of what genius?"

"Two of these nuts sucker, naw it's quarter to eleven. Why you got somewhere to be?" I asked.

"Yeah a lil later, I gotta meet my mother downtown."

"How you getting there?" I asked taking a hail of my blunt.

"I don't know, but I'll get there."

"So, when you coming back out here?"

"I don't know, but I'll make sure you know when I do!" So we smoked a blunt together, heated up a few slices of pizza left from last night and after I finished bagging up I hit the block and Rell went over her sister's house. When I got up The Wall I went up Robo's and got him to hit the block with me.

"Damn soldier, I thought y'all ain't fuck wit Robo know more, y'all ain't been by the house to say fuck you Robo or nothing."

"Yeah, shit been a lil crazy lately," I say dryly.

"I seen O ride past the other day, I said yeah my soldiers ready to re-group," Robo said with a genuine smile.

"Right here unk, I'm back out, how many?" It was going on 3 o'clock and me and Robo was almost finished the ounce. I had bagged up 188 dimes. I just counted my money and pills. It was 1520 dollars with 25 dimes's left.

"Soldier, see who that is in that car that just pulled up, they might want something." Robo said walking to the stash.

"That ain't no sale Robo, just get the two for baby girl right here".

(Honk, Honk)

Who the hell is this flagin me to their car? I say to myself as I just stare at the lone driver until she rolled down her window and said.

"What you want me to get out the car and drag you over here," Miss Fields said through her rolled down window.

"Oh shit, what you doin out here?" I say walking up to the car.

"Well, I was in the area and I remember dropping you off here so I stopped by, can you get away for a minute? I wanted to talk to you." She said seriously.

"Yeah sure, just give me a second."

I told Robo to sell the last 25 dimes for me I would be back. I told him to take 75 dollars and hold the 175 for me till I get up here. So I'm headed back to the car when..

"Ay, Scotty hold up," Vick said walking my way.

"What's up Vick, make it fast."

"I need you nephew, let me get two of em, I will pay you tonight."

"I ain't got nothing Vick, tell Robo give em to you for me."

"He out here wit your shit?"

"Naw, Vick I gotta go, I ain't fuckin wit you."

"Who was that?" Miss Fields asked when I got in the car.

"Nobody, why?"

"Cuz he looks mad, he flip'd you the finger when you walked off on em."

"Fuck him, what's up?"

"I was mostly just worried about you."

"For real, that's what's up but imma survivor, so you don't have to worry to much I should be aight."

"I know, but I have been seeing on the news all the shootings that have been going on out here, Angie told me you were okay but she was actin kinda snobby about it. How are you two doing?"

"We alright, I guess..truthfully I don't know. She..I don't think she love me like she used to."

"So what you just gave up on school?"

"You know they were gonna lock me up soon as I showed up, the year was over anyway. What we have like a month left when I stopped coming?" "Well I talked to a few of your teachers and we passed you to the 12th grade, you just have to maintain an average of at least 75 for your 12th grade year." Me and Miss Fields didn't go far, we rode to the gas station outside of Cherryhill. I don't go to our local gas station it's a death trap but anyway all in all we talked for nearly half hour then she dropped me back off and gave me a number to reach her at if I had any problems or anything. I ain't really know what I wanted to do with myself. Robo told me my mother came up here looking for me and that made me think about my lil brothers so I caught a ride out Westport and hollered at them.

"What's up big bro, I heard the police looking for you. You stabbed somebody in school?" My lil brother Jerrell asked me.

"Yeah somethin like that," I responded.

"What did you stab em for?"

"Somethin stupid, it was over a girl."

"Oh, why didn't you come out here for my birthday?"

"I'm sorry yo, I have been so caught up with my bullshit that I been neglecting y'all."

"Well you ain't miss nothing, Aunt Caroline's Jehovah's Witness so we couldn't celebrate, but we still be wanting to see you."

"I be wanting to see y'all too, I jus.. ain't no excuse really! I just gotta do better, how y'all do in school?" "We passed!" Jerrell said.

"I hate it out here, Aunt Caroline always want us to do something. Take out trash, wash dishes, then we can't never go nowhere," my other brother Tyrell complained.

"Let us come live with you, I heard you moved out of granny's house." "You hear a lot to be 13, look imma see what I can do but things are a lil dangerous right now out there and I don't think it would be safe." I stayed for a few hours with my brothers then gave them a hundred dollars and told them to split it before I left. I promised I would be back when I can.

CHAPTER 25'S INTRO

As the week ended I was feeling good, I was selling an ounce of coke every other day and didn't have to touch any of my coke money because I still had weed so whenever I wanted food, an E-pill or something I would just sell some weed and spend that money. Rell spent the last two nights with me and im really starting to feel shorty. I've been coming in early these last couple of nights, telling Rose to tell anybody who's looking for me im not here except for Glenn. Shorty had me open and I didn't even know it at the time, well not until Glenn pointed out all the changes in me. I felt, I don't know how I felt but I felt some type of way because I didn't say anything to Glenn about what Chardae said but then I was thinking why did she tell me and not Glenn. She made the situation complicated by making me the middle man when she could have told Glenn herself. If nothing else that shit had me looking at Greezy in a different way. Sexy ain't show me no disloyal signs, I heard stories of how he use to be a few years back but all he did was showed me love so that's all I could judge him by. Him and that teacher bitch was getting more serious. Me and him were on the same shit going in the house early to be with our bitch's but like I said everything was going good. Me and O were on our way to my house so I could give him the money from the last ounce I sold, when "wurp wurp".

CHAPTER 25
-You got a light-

"Fuck no, don't pull over, I got this damn gun on me!" I told O in a panic.

"Give it here," O said.

I obliged and O pulled the woodgrain panel off from the bottom of his door then slid the 380 in there and snapped the panel back on. "You know I got a warrant, I think I do anyway." I told O.

"Just give em a fake name, everything straight they shouldn't even fuck with you".

"License and registration!" The officer said standing at the driver's window.

"What's the problem?" O said thru a partially rolled down window.

"Just do as your told buddy, now pass the damn license and registration to me, before I come and get it".

"This chump tough as shit," O said more so to me then to the chump. "That's when the officer mouthed something into his walkie talkin then said.

"Okay outta the car buddy, you wanna be an asshole, well lets be assholes." A few minutes later 3 more police cars pulled up one who conveniently was apart of the warrant task force and had my picture in his car with him, which lead to my arrest for a 1st degree attempt murder and a handful of lesser charges. I was processed at Central Bookings and given a $75,000 dollar bail. I know shit was a lil tougher now a days than it had been a few months ago but niggaz act like they couldn't come up with the money. Luckily at bail review a judge reduced it to $35,000 and I had

2600 in the house of my own. I had a thousand I was about to get for O and I still have a quarter pound of weed left.

"Just put your fucking shoulder on the door, it shouldn't take much to get in". I said to Glenn while he was on the phone at Rose's house. "Rose said you goin to pay for her door." Glenn said back thru the phone. "Tell her my father will fix that shit and tell her I need her to sign for me."

"She said is there anyone else who could sign for you, because her father is in the hospital and she really needs to get there and see him."

"Oh, well tell her to go and handle her business I will get somebody to sign".

"Aight, she said she loves you and she'll see you when you get out." "Aight, tell her I love her too. Yo get the rest of my money and that weed out of there when you leave I will get that shit from you when I get out."

"Aight"

Glenn took care of everything and I got out about 1 o'clock that morning. I took about an hour to find a cab that would stop for a young nigga at that time of night, and four days at Central Bookings had me looking rough, so I know that didn't help. Anyway the cab took me to my neighborhood and took me to find Glenn so I could get a couple bags of weed. I got two for me and two for the cab driver, I went in the house and found out I was home alone. So I ran some bath water with alcohol in it, rolled up a blunt, sat in the bathtub and smoked my blunt. Halfway through it I grabbed the phone from on the side of the tub and called Angie.

"I ain't think you would be woke ugly," I said to Angie through the phone.

"Well why you call if you didn't think I would be up?"

"I took a shot!"

"Well I ain't heard from you in a week and you just decide to take a shot as you call it."

"Man, I was locked the fuck up all week, at one point & time if you ain't heard from me in 24 hours you would call the jail & hospital to check for me."

"Yeah, now I just figure you with another bitch so I don't call around."
"That's fucked up, cause I was locked up for trying to prove my love for you and you don't even care."

"Don't try to put me in that shit, ain't nobody tell you to stab that boy."

"Right, I should of just let him keep pushing up on you, you probably would of gave em some."

"Yeah, I guess it takes a cheater to know a cheater."

"What the fuck is that suppose to mean?"

"Look, did you call here to argue with me?" She asked sounding a little drained.

"No, I called to let you know where I've been at for the last week. I see you don't give a fuck though so my fault for waisting your time." I said then hung up.

The next morning I didn't wake up until a little after two when I heard Bean outside banging on the door and yelling through the mailbox.

"Scotty I know you in there boy! Open the door for I come through the window!" Bean yelled through the mail slot.

"Nigga goin get a fuckin peek hole in his forehead he climb in this window." I say opening the door for Bean.

"What's up?"

"What's up?"

"What you was in here laid up?" Bean asked after we exchanged greetings.

"Hell no! I was in here sleep, I ain't slept on a real mattress in 4 days shorty I was out."

"What's up man, you know the day my birthday and im tryin to spend it with my niggaz."

"Happy Birthday my nigga, fuck you trying to do? Im fucked up after having to pay that bail."

"Yeah Yo I ain't even find out you was locked up to last night when I ran into Glenn, he said you was good though. I took him and your mother down the Bail Bondsman to pay your bail."

"Good lookin, what you was trying to do anyway?

"Im supposed to be going to Six Flags wit Sheeky and them Saturday."

"Sheeky? That's shorty that was in the car you was talking to."

"Yeah!"

"Saturday, that's a couple days away, ya birthday today what we goin do today?" I asked.

"I don't know, we could go down the strip club," Bean says lighting my half of blunt I had in the ashtray.

"I ain't really got no money for that shit, but it's ya birthday we gonna make something happen".

Bean took me to find Glenn so I could get my weed & money. We found him over Chardae's house, so we sat around Chardae's and bagged up my quarter pound of weed. We bagged up 86 dime's, Glenn said he was going to give his lil man 75 of those dimes and he would give me 500 and tell his lil man keep 250 which was cool. We chilled out around Chardae's until the sun started to go down then we went down the hill to see who was going to the strip club with us.

Me and Bean ended up riding together in his Thunderbird with Tyrod and Glenn behind us the Cadi truck. Tyrod's rich bitch got a Cadi truck and she be kicking my man them keys out but anyway we get on Baltimore street where all the strip clubs and prostitute's are. Instead of circling the block for two parking space's we parked in the pay to park it wasn't nothing but $10 to park there all night but we should be gone in a few hours.

"I hope this bitch ain't working tonight." I said as we approached the club.

"Well why we goin to the club where she work at if you don't wanna see her?" T-Rod asked.

"This the only club we can get in without ID's!"

Inside the club I saw about 15 bitch's periodically spread around the club making their rounds. I scanned the club for my stripper bitch or what use to be my stripper bitch I didnt see her so I approached the bar and got a drink for me and Bean. It was about 7 niggaz in there other than us so we found a lil booth and kicked back and let the bitch's come to us. After being in there for about 20 minute's we attracted stripper's to entertain each of us at our booth. I was sitting at the end of the booth with a stripper that resembled Nia Long belly dancing right in front of me. As I put 5's and 1's in her bra or g-string letting my hands caress her body in the process until..

"Excuse me, can I talk to you for a minute?" My use to be stripper bitch said appearing out of nowhere.

"I ain't come to know strip club to talk and I'm kinda busy right now. .home wrecker!" I say sliding a ten in Nia Longs g-string sliding my fingers up her coochie lips.

"Home wrecker, that bitch called me. Don't blame me cause you can't keep your girl in check."

"Man, I was sleep but that ain't the point, you shoulda lied for me, told her you was my cousin or something."

"Maybe I didn't wanna lie about us!" She said, her honesty catchin me off guard.

"Aight, well maybe I don't wanna talk, it's my man birthday im chillin yo."

"So that's what it is?" She said with a threatening tone.

"Is that what what is?! I said getting annoyed.

"Come talk to me in the bathroom." She pleaded with her eyes.

"Naw im good, im chillin right here wit my niggaz and my new friend Nia Long." I said and signaled the barmaid for another drink. Shorty walked back into the changing room and that was that. A lil over an hour later we were leaving the club and as im about to head out the door my instinct had me look back only to see my used to be stripper bitch in the door of the changing room and we locked eyes for a brief moment and it seem's like for that moment I could read her mind because I swear I heard a voice say "I hate you bitch!" But I shook it off as I bumped shoulders with one of the three niggaz coming in the club, "Excuse me G" I say respectfully then continue out.

"Yo, y'all see that nigga watch us walk to the whips?" T-Rod asked.

"Who?" I asked a little tipsy.

"Look he actin like he gettin on the pay phone, you see him right there."

"Yo he was comin in the club when we was leaving out".

"You sure?"

"Yeah I bumped into the nigga."

"Look, look, he getting in that car right there."

"Fuck is that a Park Avenue?"

"Yeah, it just pulled up and he got in there."

"Let's follow em."

"Man fuck them niggaz, im strapped yall strapped so if them niggaz want some trouble, they can get it!"

On our way back to the hood we stopped at the 7 Eleven that's just outside of our hood.

"Yo, im supplying the weed, I ain't buyin the blunts too." I said as we walked in 7 Eleven.

"It's my birthday, I shouldn't have to buy nothing." Bean said.

"Let me get two boxes of Vanilla Dutch's," T-Rod says walking to the counter.

"No drinking in the store, you pay first," the foreigner says from behind the counter as im gulping Gatorade in the middle of the isle.

"Man shut up, pay for this too T-Riggy," I say as I see T-Rod already at the counter paying for his items.

"Take out for the gatorade too," Tyrod says.

"Yo y'all seen that?" Glenn asked.

"Seen what?"

"A car just pulled up on the side of the store, it look like the car that nigga from the strip club had got in but I ain't sure!" Glennn said looking thru the store window then hastly saying, "Let me see the nina right fast."

"I left that bitch in the truck."

"Bean you got cha joint on you?"

"I keep that what's up?"

"Watch that corner when we come out, matter fact have the joint out." Glenn instructed.

We walked out to the car and truck, I was a little noid (Noid:paranoid) but I ain't see the car so I thought Glenn might have been tripping. But when we came out of the door two niggaz were standing on the side of the store at the pay phone looking shakey.

"Ayo you got a light?" One of the niggaz at the phone asked.

"Yeah, here!"

Boom! Boom! Bo Bo Boom! Boom!

Pop! Pa Pa Pop! Pop! Pop!

CHAPTER 26'S INTRO

Four days after the shooting at the 7 Eleven Tyrod was able to leave the hospital. The doctor told him to come back immediately if he had any problems but other than that he should come back in 10 days to have his stitches and staples removed. He caught a bullet in the back while running to the truck. The doctor had to cut open his right chest to remove the bullet. Bean got grazed across his head, the bullet didn't actually puncture his skin, but it got so close to his head that the speed of and the head from the bullet burned a part over his left ear. All in all me and my niggaz was good, it was the other niggaz who caught the shit end of stick. Bean's return fire was enough to get the niggaz off our ass and give Glenn time to get to the truck and grab his Beretta and empty all eleven shots into there car as they tried to flee. The driver died on the scene and the passenger died a few hours later at the hospital. I think O mad at me cuz I told em I spent that stack I owe him on my bail. I don't know if he knew I was lying and that's why he was mad or if it was about the money. Either way I feel like it was partially his fault I got locked up so why shouldn't he put something to it. Plus that's all the money I had to my name was the stack I owed him. Not to mention that after staying in the house these last couple of days with Rell doing nothing but getting high and ordering out that stack is only 700 dollars now. I called the nigga Whoodie and this how that went.

CHAPTER 26
Welcome To The Club!

"What's up Whoo, you straight pimp?" I asked through the phone.

"Yeah, I just got back straight Scotty, you needa see me?"

"Yeah, I need a lil help though."

"What kinda help? You already owe me a hunnit."

"Yeah I know, im trying get the same thing I got last time."

"What you got the same amount you had last time?"

"Naw, two less."

"Goddamn, you killin me Scotty."

"I got you tho pimp, you know I just had to pay a couple stacks for this bail or I wouldn't even be comin like this."

"When you want it shorty, you ready for me now?"

"Naw, give me a couple hours imma see if Glenn trying do somethin too."

"Aight."

"Aight."

"Rell you stayin in here? I gotta make a couple of runs!" I said after I hung up the phone.

"Do you want me to stay? I've been here for three days, I know you getting tired of me."

"Naw I like you being here, especially since Rose ain't been back, I hate being in the house by myself."

"So you just using me?" Rell said jokingly.

"Naw, I fucks wit you."

(Rinnng, Rinnng, Rinnng)

"Hello",

"Hey Scotty, I got some bad news," Rose said thru the phone.

"What's wrong Rose?"

"My father passed this morning."

"Oh wow, im sorry to hear that."

"It's okay, im okay my moms taking it a little hard though so imma stay with her for a while and I need you to take care of the house out there."

"Sure, anything you need Rose."

"Alright, I knew I could count on you Scotty."

"Aight, take care and give my condolence's to your mother." I said then we hung up.

After talking to Rose I took a shower and went to see T-Rod.

"How you feelin Rod?" I asked walking up on his porch.

"I feel like a dope fiend, I have been pumping oxy-cottons in me since last night and before that they had me hooked to a machine. All I had to do was press a button ande Morphine was pumped into my system instantly."
"Fuck you complaining about, you've been getting high for free all week!" I say joking.

"Tyrod your food ready baby," some thick diva said sticking half of her body out the door.

"Did you roll the blunt for me?" Tyrod asked the diva.

'Yeah, it's right here."

"Come here, this Scotty, Scotty this is Shantae she the one I been telling you about."

"What's up."

"What's up."

"Tae you wanna tell Scotty the good news."

"I'm having Tyrods baby Scotty and me and Tyrod are making you the godfather."

"Wow, that is good news, well congratulations and im honored."

"You hungry?" Shantae asked, "I cooked home fries, sausage, and scrambled eggs with cheese."

"If I wasn't before, I am now!" I said with a smile.

"Alright then, I will make y'all plates," Shantae said then went back in the house.

"Damn, you got a winner Rod, is that the one with the money?"

"Yeah that's my baby, you like her?"

"She seem cool, what she say about you bleeding everywhere in her truck?"

"She ain't say shit, yo while I was laid up for them couple of days in the hospital my mind started wandering."

"Wanderin about what?"

"About who shot me or why he shot me rather and I come to the conclusion one of them strippers put the niggaz on us. Either your old bitch or one of the bitch's we was chillin wit. I think the niggaz was goin to try and rob us but they wasn't expecting us to be strapped."

"That bitch was looking at me crazy when we was leavin out, she was just staring at me."

"Which one?"

"My use ta be stripper bitch."

"That bitch put them niggaz on us!"

"What you wanna do?"

"Y'all plates on the table," Shantae said coming back to the door.

"Come on, let's eat we will figure that shit out later."

After we ate me and T-Rod sat out front smoking and enjoying the weather. It was about one in the afternoon when Keyco pulled up.

"What's up wit chall niggaz?" Keyco said as he walked up on the porch.

"Aw man, we just chillin enjoying the day." I said non-chalantley.

"Where you comin from?" T-Rod asked Keyco.

"Up the shopping center! Oh I saw Angie up there too Scotty, wat y'all beefin?"

"Fuck her, what she say?"

"Same thing you just said, I asked her what was up wit you and she said fuck him that jerk hung up on me."

"For real fuck her, what's up wit Jah?" I asked.

"That nigga outta town, he should be back next week." Keyco said.

"You think he still trying to fuck wit me on that blow tip?"

"I don't see why not, I will holla at him soon as he get back."

I set out there and rapped with Keyco and T-Rod for about a half hour maybe forty five minutes that's when Greezy's Crown Vic pulled up.

"If it ain't the dynamic duo," I say slappin hands with Sexy and Big Greezy.

"Where the pills at?" Greezy asked.

"I've been down here for about an hour and I ain't seen Del or Tommy."

"Ay D-Roy!" Sexy yelled up at the window.

"Damn it feel good as shit our here," Tommy said as he came out the door blowing out cigarette smoke.

We all, well me, Greezy and Sexy brought E-pills then we went around the corner to Ki-Ki's house to holler at Poka. We tripped with Ki-Ki and Tywanda while we waited for Poka to get out of the shower and our pills to kick in. KiKi had a little over a half of fifth of Bacardi dark rum down there so with our pills in us we sipped on that and before I knew it, it was 3:30, I think to myself as P-olie walks through the door of Poka's house.

"I can't fuckin believe this shit!" P said pouring the last corner of Bacardi in a plastic cup.

"Calm down, what's wrong P?" Poka said.

"You ain't goin believe this shit!" P exclaimed.

"Just tell me what the fuck happened!"

"I come home from work and my whole apartment is trashed with the door unlocked an all that."

"Fuck no."

"Look at my face do I look like I'm joking?"

"What you ain't lock the door before you left out?"

"Yeah I locked the fuckin door, a nigga came through the back window, you know my apartment on the bottom floor and ain't nothing but woods out back."

"What they get?"

"Everything!"

"Everything?"

"The whole 11 and half ounces, the bitch ass niggaz even took my playstation".

"How they find the coke?" Poka asked growing upset.

"I don't know they looked for it, I had it in a cereal box on top of the fridgerator."

"Who you think.."

"Fuck no!" Poka roared slapping a cup off the table.

My pill was in full effect so my mind was wandering, at first I was mad that someone broke into P's house. Then I thought these niggaz got all this coke and ain't put nothing to my bail, man fuck their coke. I mean im still gonna rock out when we find out who stole it but right now this pill is startin to kick my ass. I called up Rose's because I started thinking about Rell and my E-pill had me feeling freaky but no one answered so I called over her sister's house and she told me Rell had just got in a cab to go up their mother's house but Glenn was on Jennifer's porch and wanted to talk to me.

"Take Glenn the phone Nae," I said.

"I'm already on the porch I don't have to take him the phone."

"Let me holla at em."

"Why you sound like that?" Nae asked.

"Give me the phone Nae." I heard Glenn say in the background.

"Scotty!"

"What it is G?"

"Bitch you got a pill in you," Glenn said in a whisper".

"Yup!"

"Where you at yo?"

"Down Poka spot."

"I'm on my way!"

"Don't snatch it no more punk!" I heard Nae tell Glenn in the background before the phone hung up.

Glenn got down the hill in record time.

"What you flew down this bitch?" I asked Glenn as he walked in the house.

"If it ain't one thing it's a mufuckin nother," Glenn said sniffing a quarter filled cup of Bacardi on the table then downing it.

"What's the matter?" I say dispassionately, not that I didn't care I just thought he was ready to say the police was looking for us or some shit like that.

"My fuckin lil man got locked up and I just hit em off this morning."

"Well join the fuckin club." Poka said dryly.

"What club?"

"The, I just took the lost club."

"Damn so you fucked up too and I just talked to Whoodie this mornin, he said he just got back straight." I said.

"Oh yeah, nigga rob his bitch ass".

"Rob who bitch ass?" Sexy asked coming from upstairs out the bathroom.

"The nigga Whoodie."

"The weed nigga?"

"Yeah."

"Y'all think he holdin?"

"Thers only one way ta find out!"

Now I wasn't really wit robbing Whoodie cause I ain't no stick-up-boy, that ain't my thing but my niggaz come before everybody except family. So fuck it, if I had to make a choice to see Whoodie fucked up or my nig-gaz fucked up..ain't no choice. I did kinda manipulate the situation to the point that we wouldn't have to actually full blast the nigga. Cause I know my niggaz, they was goin kill him after they got the weed and money so I told my niggaz I was going to call Whoodie to meet me and sell me a pound and while that was going on they could just break in his house and steal the money and weed.

"Yo I just talked to him, he meeting me at Vick's house so go head. He said he's in the house so y'all should see em leave or if his car ain't out there you already know."

"Aight."

"Aight."

"What's up Whoo?"

"What it is shorty?"

"Aw man, im just tryin ta maintain until shit cool down up The Wall." I said honestly.

"Yeah you can pretty much keep a low profile selling weed.. Ay get in matter of fact Whoodie said lookin at his pager.

I got in Whoodie's silver 96 Lexus LS 400 and he passed me his blunt then started talking.

"Yeah like I was saying, you can stay low key sellin weed. I've been selling this shit for the last 3 years and I ain't been locked up once." Whoodie said.

"That's a nice lil run," I responded.

"Yeah cause weed customers ain't like crack customers, you know crack heads look like they buying drugs but weed customers..like now. It look like me and you just hanging out, we ain't drawing no attention to each other".

"Yeah, I see what you sayin." I said passing him his blunt back.

"You busy? Ride wit me right quick." He said.

"Where we goin?"

"I wanna run down my house and grab something for my brother 50 right quick."

"Your house?" I say a little hesitant but he never been this inviting before.

"Yeah imam be in and out."

"Aight umm, just stop me past the shopping center so I can grab a water, my mouth dry as shit." I say trying to buy Sexy and them some time.

"A water, aw man I got a fridgerator full of Deer Parks," he said and pulled off from in front of Vick's house.

5 minutes later we pulled up in front of Whoodie's house.

"Come on, you can come in," Whoodie said as we were getting out of the car.

As we approached the front door nothing looked out of place but I suspect them niggaz had enough sense not to go in through the front door since the view of the front was so much broader than the backs. We enter through the kitchen and soon as we get in there and shut the door we heard a door or draw shut and a sneaker squeak upstairs.

"SSSH!" Whoodie said and grabbed a revolver out his kitchen cabinet and inched to the stairwell, then peaked up the stairs. He then took a step back and put his index finger to his closed lips indicating for me to keep quiet. A few seconds later we heard footsteps coming down the steps as the foot steps approached the bottom of the flight of stairs Whoodie began to raise his revolver.

"What the fuck!" Sexy said raising his gun.

"Bet not shoot me bitch," I said putting a lil more pressure into my bear hug.

"Let the gun go," Sexy demanded to Whoodie as he raised his gun to Whoodie's head.

"Oh shit look who's here," Glenn said coming down the steps with Greezy behind him.

"Good this bitch can open this safe for us, I thought we was goin to have to take this mufucka wit us," Greezy said.

"Come on upstairs!" Sexy commanded Whoodie and then handed me the gun he took from Whoodie.

Upstairs Whoodie opened the safe and we filled one pillow case with weed and another with money, then Glenn put his gun to the back of Whoodie's head.

"Please, y'all got the weed and the money please don't kill me..please!"

"Yeah you know, I don't really want to but I got to Whoodie. I can't go around watching my back for the rest of my life cause I let you live. That's just not how shit works." Glenn said.

"I swear, I'll just take it as a lost. I ain't coming after y'all, not even you Scotty. Fuck the weed, fuck the money, just let me live please."

"Scotty find something to tie around your face, we about to get outta here." Sexy told me.

"Yo I don't think imma leave wit y'all a few people seen me come in with him. So I'm just goin run out the front and y'all go out the back".

"You sure?" Glenn asked me.

"I'm probably going have to, fuck it I ain't goin have no gun powder on my hands what the fuck the police goin to do. I'll tell em a nigga wit a mask on grabbed yo and I ran out the door."

"Aight if that's how you wanna play it."

"Yeah, I think it's best," I said and took a last look at Whoodie who appeared to be saying a prayer to hisself before..Boom!Boom!

CHAPTER 27'S INTRO

This year took a nigga for a ride, 2001 a year I'll probably never forget, even if I tried my R.I.P Fezie tattoo wouldn't let me. The police knocking Fezie off his bike, him breaking his neck due to the fall and us standing over his body when the paramedic said he was gone. I think we all died a little that day. I heard the saying before what a difference a day makes, how true that is. Not only the day Fezie died but me and Angie's valentine's day rendezvous. It seem like that day started off perfect and ended anything but that, not to mention that lead to me being shot at for the first time in my life and not only shot at but grazed. The way those feathers flew up out my coat I thought my goose was cooked. I'm missing my nigga Manna too, I was just thinking about how he had me stunting at the mall. I never fucked that bitch Tarsha neither, Jennifer's party at Patapsco Arena was off the chain until they locked my niggaz up, that really fucked that night up. Fucking Marie did a little justice for that night, but it still ain't even out. Reem crazy ass taking over that was like switching coachs in the middle of the season but Pelle Pelle did that to himself playing games. Damn I should have went and hollered at my foreign friend whos store I got jumped in, he probably would have been a good customer on the weed tip. I was asking myself did I do the right thing in not taking sides when Glenn shot Jah and I think I did because I still feel the same way about it. I know one thing that stripper bitch had some good pussy and she knew how to use it. That's crazy cuz good pussy can kill niggaz cuz I don't wanna believe it was her who sent them niggaz at us. Probably cuz I still want to fuck her! It's crazy cuz in 2000 I ain't even eat pussy but here it is

01 and im E-pilled up licken a stripper bitch's ass, not now I'm just think-ing about that night at the hotel. I'm sitting here eating this Spaghetti thinking that nigga Tommy made the best Spaghetti I ever tasted, when..

CHAPTER 27
Booked

"Ray! You got a visit," the correctional officer yelled down the hall.

Yeah I'm booked, not at bookings neither I have been thru that process already and since I was given a $150,000 bail I think im going to be here for a minute. Niggaz wasn't even trying to pay a $75,000 now I got double that, I don't stand a chance. Anyway I've been down for going on a month and now I'm sitting in the same visiting room I went to see O and Row at over city jail. I'm in my assigned seat waiting for my visitor to come in and sit down and surprisingly it was..

"Rell, what are you doing here yo?" I asked expecting to see one of my niggaz but happy to see a female that isn't wearing a blue uniform and she had Jennifer with her.

"I thought you'd be happy to see me."

"I am, I just wasn't expecting to."

"Well who were you expecting?"

"I don't know, Sexy, Greezy, one of my niggaz to show love."

"You don't call Rose house or your grandmother's?"

"I called a few people the first week but lately I been on some chill shit. Niggaz know where I'm at, I shouldn't have to hunt them down." "Well you are right about that cuz they'll be over here to join you. The police locked Sexy, Greezy, and Glenn up last week. Greezy crashed his car trying to get away, you ain't hear about that?"

"Hell no, what they lock em up for?"

"I heard for killing some boy in a house or something."

I just sat there dazed for a minute thinking how the fuck did they charge them, the way the police harassed me about the shit. I figured I was their only lead. Fuckin homicide badgered me for 16 hours hoping I would slip up but we went over that shit to many times I had my story down packed. It wasn't shit I could do about them raiding my spot and finding my weed at least it wasn't no gun in my house at the time.

"Scotty! snap out of it, you ain't even going to speak," Jennifer said.

"Damn my bad, what's up Jennifer, that shit just crazy, I wanna talk to them niggaz."

"Well Glenn called me after he saw the commissioner; he said all of em got no bails."

We talked for almost the rest of the 45 minute visit about this and that, hood gossip, me and Rell's first night together and then the first night we actually fucked. She said she raped me, I guess it was about five minutes left when shit got real.

"So when you think you coming home?" She asked.

"It should be in a couple of months or so, I don't think the nigga coming to court to press charges about the attempt murder and if they throw that out I might can get probation for the weed," I said then asked "why?" sensing it was more to her question.

"Do you miss me?"

"Yeah, I miss you and I know you probably want to be home to see your baby born."

"Baby, by who?"

"By me silly she said standing up showing her stomach."

"You don't look pregnant to me."

"I'm only 6 weeks."

I was a little distraught when I got back to my cell, I know from hood experiences when most niggaz are approached by females claiming their pregnant by them the first thing the guy says is "It ain't mines"

but I know I didn't use condoms with Rell even though we only fucked a handful of times. I know it only takes one so maybe it was mines.

The city jail is composed of sections that are labeled from A-Z, each section houses roughly 120 inmates two to each cell usually. I was being housed on J section. My cell buddy was coo, l a East Baltimore dude named Pistol Pete. He taught me the ropes, all the do's and don't's in jail. He was in his late 20's but he's been in and out of prison all his life. About a week and a half after Rell had come to see me I was getting use to being here or at least the way things worked. Then one morning on my way to the shower, I walked past a cell and saw a familiar face.

"What's up boy?" I said excitedly looking at Glenn like I ain't seen him in years.

"What it is, I was hoping they put me on the same section as you."

"Yeah Rell told me they locked y'all up, how the fuck they..what the fuck happened?"

"I don't even know for real, once I get my motion I will see what's what, but my charge papers don't say shit."

"Where Sexy and Greezy?"

"Sexy on K section, they sent Greezy upstairs on N section."

"You get 15 minutes to shower and the clock started ticking when I opened your cell. If you waist your 15 minutes talking don't think your getting a shower," some female correctional officer told me.

"I'm good," I said waving her off.

"You said Rell came to see you?"

'Yeah her and Jennifer came down here, why Rell trying to put a baby on me!"

"What she say?"

"She said she was pregnant."

"And what did you say?"

"I ain't know what to say."

"Might be, y'all was laid up all the time."

"Yeah it might be."

"Oh yo, I seen Lil Greezy on my way down to medical, he hollered at you."

Oh yeah, how his case looking?"

"He said they threw out the attempt murder but they're charging him with the gun and the police are saying he pointed the gun at them before he ran and threw it."

"Hell no they would have of shot his ass."

"Right, he said they said if he plead out to 5 years for the gun they won't charge him with assault on a police officer."

"When the fuck he assault them?"

"They said when he pointed the gun that was assault on the officer."

"Them bitches playing dirty."

I know I was locked up but while me and Glenn were together it didn't feel like that. We talked days away like it was nothing, Glenn knew Jennifer's address and by Nae (Rell's sister) living next door I sent a letter to Jennifer's house for Rell about a week ago. In the letter I told Rell to get some things out of Rose's house and put them up for me. No guns or drugs just clothes and my Playstation I sent to my little brothers. I had her find Ms. Fields number and give it to me in her letter when she wrote back, which im still waiting for her letter which I should get any day. Me and Glenn were in the rec room playing spades against some niggaz when..

"Ray, you got mail!" the correctional officer yelled to me.

I was expecting it to be from Rell but it was a letter from granny.

Dear Jamal,

I hope this letter reaches you in the very best of health. I am writing because you haven't called in over a month and I'm wondering is everything alright. I know you can take care of yourself but we still worry when we don't hear from you. I hope you make use of your time in there. Do you have a bible? If not you should get one and read it. I know GOD has a plan for you and maybe this is just his way of slowing you down so you can see what the plan is. Me and your grandfather sent you 50 dollars we will try to send you 50 dollars monthly. Take care, Love Granny

Two days later I got a letter from Rell

Dear Scotty,

I got your letter and I did everything you asked I had Robo carry your clothes down your grandmother's house. I also had him take the Playstation to your grandmother with the instructions that is was for your little brothers. I saw that name you were talking about Tamika Fields with her phone number, don't be mad but I ripped it up. I don't want my baby father having to depend on another bitch, so whatever you needed her to do I will do. I went to the clinic for a check-up everything is fine with the baby by the time you get this letter I should be going on 9 weeks pregnant. Me and my mother got into it so im staying with my sister you can write and I'll write back. I will be to see you as soon as I can. Do you love me? You don't have to tell me right away but I think I love you. Rell

P.S. I didn't tell your family that I was pregnant seeing that you didn't but I feel you will when your ready! (smiley face)

"Shorty crazy as shit Scotty," Glenn said reading the letter after me. "Far as I know she ain't no bad girl, she ain't got no real fucked up track record like some of these bitches out the way."

The next morning around 10:30 me and Glenn were called up to visiting room. While were walking up there we were in the hall talking. Glenn said it was probably Jennifer and Rell because homeboys don't really visit niggaz in the joint it be the bitch's that beat the doors down, but it was O and Reem.

"What's up wit chall niggaz," O said as we exchanged hand greetings.

"We chill's, hoping these court dates hurry up and roll around." I said.

"Did you get your motion yet Glenn?"

"Naw, I'm waiting to see what's in them though cause I know they ain't got shit."

"Manna hollered at y'all niggaz too," Reem said.

"He home?"

"Naw the juvenile spot let him out on a weekend pass but he gone back now," he said he should be home in November.

"Y'all open The Wall back up yet?"

"Naw Poka & P-olie still doing their thing down by Ki-Ki's house and been doing something around Hillside."

"So what y'all ain't doing nothing?"

"Me and Reem been hitting a couple of weight sales but I've been study trying to get these CDL's."

"You still on that shit!" I asked.

"I told you shorty, it's money in that shit and whereever the money at you going find me," O exclaimed.

"I hear that shit."

"What about Row, why you ain't get him to come back out wit you," Glenn asked.

"Ever since we came home off that body Row been on some other shit, I heard he got a job at Wal-mart or somewhere."

"I feel him, he ain't want no more parts of this mufucka," I said referring to the jail.

We rapped about everything we could think of until the visit was over then we told each other we loved one another then they (O and Reem) left and we went back to our section.

CHAPTER 28'S INTRO

The state took Sexy, Glenn, and Big Greezy to trial 5 months later at their first scheduled trial date. They would not grant them a postponement and the judge let the state's attorney get away with all kinds of shady tricks. The state found two witnesses against them. One woman who was supposedly sitting in her car and saw the three of them run out of the house after hearing two shots fired, and a old guy who lived 2 doors down who claim he saw Greezy push the living room's air conditioner thru the window then saw Glenn jump through the window and let Sexy and Greezy in the house. He didn't say why he didn't call the police after he saw this. Plus even if he did see that it still shouldn't have been enough for a conviction because he didn't see anybody kill Whoodie so how can you find them guilty of murdering Whoodie and you didn't see the murder. You just saw them go in the house the murderer could have already been in the house or anything but needless to say it was enough for this judge and jury because they were all found guilty and sentenced to life plus 20 years. That hurt, im still fighting my cases and they act like they can't find my victim. Whos problem is that? But the judge keeps letting them postpone my case to try and find him. Rell stomach looks like it's about to bust open as she walks towards me to take a seat in the visiting room.

CHAPTER 28

Let tomorrow worry about tomorrow!

"That smile looks forced, is everything okay, is the baby okay?" I asked her.

"Yeah, the baby's fine," she responded.

"Well what's wrong?"

"Do you love me?"She asked.

"I don't like the sound of that but yeah, you know I love you, you showed me more love than anybody since I been in here."

"Do you love me no matter what?"

"Come on now Rell wit this shit, what did you do? Spit it out."

"Do you remember when we first started messing around and I would go and visit my mother for a week or so?"

"Yeah I remember."

"Well she wasn't the only one I was visiting."

"I kinda figured that but we weren't together together so I ain't try to regulate your whereabouts."

"I know and that made me like you even more, but I have the baby next month and I love you so much that I can't lie to you anymore."

"It's not my baby?" I ask.

"It's..It's..I don't know if it is or it isn't, it could be yours or it could be his."

"Why you just telling me this shit?"

"I don't know, I was scared..I messed up! Please don't be mad, im sorry."

"I ain't mad, I just..I just don't wanna talk to you right now," I said and walked out of the visiting room.

After leaving the visiting room I went back to my cell and laid in my bunk. I was mad, but I wasn't mad that the kid might not have been mine because when she got pregnant she wasn't my girl. It ain't like she cheated on me or nothing, im mad that I told my family and my niggaz im about to have a son and now it turns out I might not be. I guess im mad because I feel like I got played and that lead me to play my niggaz and my family they brought baby clothes, strollers, and all that shit. Now I might not even have a baby coming. The more I thought about it the madder I became.

"Scotty! Scotty!" My cell buddy snapped me out of my daze.

"Yo!" I snapped.

"Here nigga, grab your tray."

"I don't want this shit, go head".

"You don't want none of it?"

"Naw, I'm good."

"You aight my nigga? You've been zoned out since you came off of that visit."

"Yo, I don't even feel like talking bout dat shit right now," I said and went back into my daze.

I lost track of time but I know I laid there for every bit of 5 hours without moving or speaking until.

"Ray! Attorney visit," the correctional officer yelled to me.

I don't even remember the walk to the attorney visiting room, it's like my mind was blank. It's just like my feet were moving mechanically while my brain was still in lala land.

"How are you doing Mr. Ray?" My lawyer asked as I came in and took a seat.

"What difference do it make," I said rudely.

"I guess none when you put it that way."

"What's up? I'm trying get back to my cell."

"Okay well let's get to business, I have some good news and some bad news, which one do you want first?"

"Give me the bad," I say.

"The bad news is the victim in your attempt murder case was found and the police have him in their custody trying to get him to testify."

"Okay, so what's the good news?"

"I talked with the states attorney this morning and I got her to come down on her plea offer."

"Come down to what?"

"Well before she was offering 10 years for the attempt murder alone."

"Okay so now what's she talking?"

"I talked her down to 5 years for a joint plea."

"What the fuck is that?"

"You'll plead to 5 years for the attempt murder and 3 years for possession with the intent to distribute marijuana."

"5+3 is 8 and I ain't trying to do no jail time, I been told you that."

"Well..you're doing jail time and you'd be doing the 5 years and the 3 years at the same time so the 5 would eat up the 3 and I can recommend you for the youth offenders program and if you complete it you'll be out in another 18 months".

"Did you interview the victim for the attempt murder? I don't think he's going to cooperate with the police."

"No I haven't interviewed him yet but regardless of what he does now they have his original statement and they'll try to trick him up on the stand. It's a gamble, if you get found guilty they'll give you 25 years that's a big jump from 18 months."

"Yeah and 18 months is a big jump from immediately, I need to get home, I got shit I need to do."

"I understand that but you stabbed this damn boy in front of your whole school."

"Says who?"

"If I say I didn't and he says I didn't I don't think the jury will find me guilty. Just do me a favor, interview him see if he's still on our side then come back and see me."

This day just keeps getting better first Rell kid might not be mines now my lawyer wants me to take 5 years. I went back to my cell and cooled out. My cell buddy was in the rec room so I was alone with my thoughts. That's when I did something I haven't did since I was a kid, I prayed. After my prayer I felt at ease like a weight had been lifted, so I then opened my Bible and begun to read.

I was once told if you take a step towards the Lord and he'll take two steps towards you and I believe it because it's been a month since I first opened my Bible and I have been reading it for at least an hour out of each day and saying the Lord's Prayer before I go to sleep each night. One of the things I first started praying for was for my parents to stop getting high. Now my mother has been getting high for at least the past 10 years and I have only been praying for the last month, but today I got a money order from my mom and a letter letting me know she's been clean (Clean:Drug free) for a week. I know that's not a long time but it's a start and im happy she's making an effort. Not only that but the victim in my attempt murder case could only be held for so long and once they had to let him go he hit the ground running. My lawyer said the state doesn't have a reliable address or phone number for him and we're trying to get that case thrown out. Tomorrow I go to court for the weed they found in Rose's house when they raided it. A bunch of inmates have been telling me since my name isn't on Rose's lease the police can't charge me with the weed. That shit sound good but I have been praying on it and I will leave it up to GOD and my lawyer. It's crazy because I was a little on edge wondering how things would go tomorrow when I came across a verse in my Bible that read "Do not worry about tomorrow, for tomorrow will worry about its own things. Sufficient for the day is its own troubles." So I took heed prayed and went to sleep.

The next morning I was waken up at 5:00AM to get prepared for a 9:00AM court appearance. I was cuffed and shackled with the rest of the chain gang and transported to the courthouse's holding cell. I arrived at the court house at about 7:30AM and at about 9:30AM I was getting anxious because about 20 people had been taken up for court and I wasn't one of em. Now around 10:15 the suspense was killing me thats when I saw my lawyers cool ass strutting my way.

"I've got some good news, some bad news and some good news Mr. Ray," he says.

"Here we go again with this shit," I say about to throw a fit.

"Calm down, Calm down let me finish."

"Yeah ya ass about to be finished," I mumbled to myself thinking im about to fire this nigga.

"I heard that and that's the thanks I get for busting my ass."

"Man you said I would be home in six months now you always got bad news."

"Okay Okay, it took a little longer than I anticipated but do you want the news or not?"

"Give it to me."

"Aight, first things first the house raid is DONE!"

"What do you mean done?"

"Done, Fineto, Finished! You don't even have to go upstairs to the courtroom."

"Your kidding."

"Got it right here in writing," he says showing me some paperwork stamped case dismissed.

"Well what's the bad news?"

"I tried to get the attempt murder thrown out also but I couldn't."

"Well I don't go to court for that for another 60 days damn near," I said.

"But, I work wonders hear me out. I couldn't get the attempt murder thrown out but the states attorney was willing to drop the charges to a 1st degree assault and change the plea agreement to 10 years, all suspended but 9 and half months you have in with 3 years probation upon your release."

"So what does that mean?"

"It means if you want the deal, you go home today."

"Today?"

"What about the 10 years, 3 years whatever you just said?"

"The 10 years is suspended meaning you don't have to do it unless..you go home and get found guilty of some other charges before your 3 years probation period is up."

"So what your saying is I can go home to-day?"

"Yes!"

"I love you man, you know I was just playing about firing you and shit."

"Yeah I know, well you do have to come upstairs to sign a couple of papers and I guess that concludes our business."

EPILOGUE

I didn't call and let anybody know I was coming home, I just showed up. I caught a cab to The Wall, but nobody was there so I had the cab take me down Ki'Ki's house where I found Poka and Manna high out of their minds. Manna gave me 20 dollars to pay my cab then let me know what was going on. Him and Poka had The Wall back jumping the police ain't been buzzing like they use to, they were selling weed and crack now. They were going to New York to get weed some exotic shit called blueberry and it was doing crack numbers. Manna controlled the crack and Poka controlled the weed. They ain't been catching no heat from niggaz, nobody wanted beef. Manna said he talked to Sexy the other day and he wants him to kill the nigga Jah, he said the nigga put a $5,000 contract on him and that's like $50,000 in the joint. Rell had the baby two days ago and she's supposed to get out of the hospital tomorrow. I haven't talked to her since she visited and told me that shit, I don't know how imma play that situation. I ain't even get high wit Manna and them because I had to go see my probation officers tomorrow and I don't know if I'm going to have to get drug tested. I stayed down Poka's and went up my grandmother's house the next morning and got lectured about if I do the same things I did before I went to jail im going to get the same results. Chic took me to see my probation officer and then to get some new clothes, to see my lil brothers and my mother was over there as well. Everywhere I went everyone asked the same question!

"Now that your home what are you going to do?" I just tell em like the Bible told me I will let tomorrow worry about tomorrow! But to my readers I will tell you this..This story is far from over, so I encourage you to read book 2 of The Wallboys story entitled "Off the Wall." I promise you will not be disappointed.

Author Contacts

Facebook:Scottyfromdawall
Instagram:Scottyfromthewall
Email:jamalray1000@gmail.com

Visuals can be found on Youtube @
Wallboys Trailer
Wallboys Web trailer
Wallboys Web Series Preview